"But

"Why not? It's easy." Dylan put his hands loosely on her shoulders.

Katy shivered. "B-because I'm not in the habit of kissing just anybody."

"I'm not just anybody. I'm supposed to be your soon-to-be fiancé."

"Nevertheless, I can't put my heart into it without some emotional content."

"Emotional *what*? Look, Katy, we're just talking about a kiss here. A very simple kiss between...between friends...."

He drew her a tiny fraction closer.

"We're not friends," she managed to say. "We're... we're..."

He bent toward her. "What are we, Katy? Can't wait to see what word you come up with."

"We're—" Doomed, she thought, lifting her hands to touch the wide shoulders while his hands drifted to her waist. "We're going to put people's suspicions to rest once and for all."

Ruth Jean Dale lives in a Colorado pine forest within shouting distance of Pikes Peak. She is surrounded by two dogs, two cats, one husband and a passel of grown children and growing grandchildren. A former newspaper reporter and editor, she is living her dream: writing romance novels for Harlequin. As she says with typical understatement, "It doesn't get any better than this! Everyone should be so lucky."

Books by Ruth Jean Dale

HARLEQUIN ROMANCE®

Fiancé Wanted!
Ruth Jean Dale

HARLEQUIN®

TORONTO • NEW YORK • LONDON
AMSTERDAM • PARIS • SYDNEY • HAMBURG
STOCKHOLM • ATHENS • TOKYO • MILAN • MADRID
PRAGUE • WARSAW • BUDAPEST • AUCKLAND

ISBN 0-373-03593-4

FIANCÉ WANTED!

First North American Publication 2000.

CHAPTER ONE

BABY SHOWERS always depressed Katy Andrews.

So did wedding showers, April showers and, if she'd been able to think of any other kind of showers, they would no doubt depress her, too.

The fact was, at the advanced age of thirty, Katy had neither husband, child, nor prospects of obtaining either in the foreseeable future.

Which was the reason that sitting in the middle of pink and blue crepe-paper streamers in a corner of the Rawhide Café in Rawhide, Colorado, didn't exactly leave her brimming with enthusiasm.

That is, until her best friend Laura Reynolds waddled into the café, let out a little shriek of surprise and was immediately obscured by a horde of hugging females.

Katy sighed. Laura's baby was due in another month—late September. The glowing mother-to-be had left her job as lifestyles editor of the Rawhide *Review* newspaper six weeks ago to await the birth of this, her second child. Katy, city reporter for the *Review,* thought the place hadn't been the same without her best friend.

But she had to admit that married life agreed with Laura, who had never looked lovelier. Even minus her customary grace, she was a joy to behold as she waddled up to Katy with a big smile on her face.

Katy's answering smile was completely sincere. She might be envious of her friend's happiness, but she wouldn't be mean-spirited about it. "Long time, no see," she said.

"Too long." Laura eased herself into a chair across the table. "There just seems so much to do to get ready for the baby."

"But you've got such good help," Katy teased.

"Oh, yes," Laura agreed airily. "Just what I need—a ten-year-old girl and a seven-year-old boy 'helping.' This poor little baby will be lucky to have a *bed* when it arrives, with all that help."

Katy figured that "poor little baby" would be just about the luckiest baby around. It would arrive to find a loving blended family waiting, complete with father Matt, mother Laura, sister Jessica and brother Zach. The importance of a bed paled by comparison.

"Is Matt getting excited?" Katy wanted to know.

Laura rolled her eyes. "Deliriously. Even when I informed him that I expect him to go into the delivery room and hold my hand the entire time, he didn't run screaming from the house."

"Brave guy," Katy agreed. That her old school friend Matt would turn out to be such a rock impressed her. He was certainly nothing like his friend and Katy's long-time nemesis, Dylan Cole. Katy would have bet that you couldn't melt Dylan and pour him into a delivery room.

Laura beamed. "The kids say I owe it all to you and that magic wand they gave to you," she said with a mischievous gleam in her eyes. "They're probably right. After all, who else would have forked out hard cash for those magnificent glass slippers? They made it impossible for me to turn down the pleas of my Prince Charming.''

The two women laughed together, reliving the trials and tribulations leading up to the happy melding last year of Matt and his daughter with Laura and her son into one big happy family.

Katy had been a willing participant with the children in bringing about the union of two people obviously meant to spend their lives together. Yielding to the children's pleas, she'd bought the ugliest and biggest plastic shoes in the world for Prince Charming to slip upon the dainty feet of his Cinderella. To avoid any last-minute complications, Jessica and Zach had also made and decorated a ''magic wand'' out of a paper plate and a dowel, presenting it to Katy as their own special Fairy Godmother. Getting into the spirit of the occasion, Katy had waved that wand around with more enthusiasm than verve.

''And,'' Laura added, ''I see you've brought your wand with you today. Are we going to need a little magic?''

''Laura, I need a *lot* of magic. My family is driving me nuts about—''

''Laura, Laura, we need you at the head table.'' Rawhide's Mayor Marilyn Rogers appeared to whisk Laura away to the place of honor. Throughout the luncheon, throughout the opening of baby gifts, Katy remained uncharacteristically quiet, in the background, with a half-sad smile pasted on her face.

All this hoop-de-doo couldn't help but remind her of her own failings. Thirty and single, her entire family was on her back to marry and reproduce—as if it were that simple. She couldn't exactly wave her magic wand—as successful as it had been in the past—and conjure up a Romeo of her own.

If she could, she certainly would. A movement near the door caught her eye and she saw Dylan Cole enter. He hesitated, looking around for a table. She could only hope he didn't notice the empty one directly behind where she sat.

She and Dylan couldn't be in the same room for five minutes without launching into battle. It had been that way all their lives, even back in grammar school when he and his buddy Matt Reynolds had made her life miserable.

She turned her back on him just in time to see Laura pull a beautiful hand-made baby quilt from a brightly wrapped box. Good thing mother isn't here to see this, Katy thought darkly. Lovely and feminine, Laura was the daughter her mother *should* have had, she thought gloomily even as she applauded enthusiastically. Instead, her mother had got a daughter who grew up a wild tomboy ready to take on the world.

On her thirtieth birthday last October 25, Katy had thought her mother and grandmother were going to hold a wake. And this year, she realized, would be even worse. Her grandmother's health had deteriorated, her mother reported weekly, and Grandma's only wish was "to see Katy settled before I die."

"Settled," to the Andrews family, meant married, preferably with children.

Throughout lunch and the opening of gifts, Katy

mentally reviewed every man she knew in or near the town of Rawhide and came up short. There wasn't a single suitable husband for her in all the land—and she knew them all. Born and raised here, now in her seventh year as a reporter at the local paper, it was no exaggeration to say she knew *everyone*.

The shower wound to a close. Katy remained in her seat while Laura said her good-byes and thank-yous, then approached to sink gratefully, if ungracefully, into the chair she'd occupied earlier.

"Isn't everyone nice?" Laura gushed. "To go to so much trouble for me is just—"

"Natural," Katy inserted, "because *you're* so nice, Laura."

Laura smiled. "I don't know about that, but I do know that I'm so happy I sometimes think I'm just going to burst with it." Leaning across the table, she patted Katy's hand. "In fact, I'm so happy that I want all my friends to share in it. Lately, I've been getting this uncontrollable urge to play matchmaker. Isn't that awful?"

"Start with me," Katy said fervently. "Laura, my mom and grandmother are driving me nuts. They're after me constantly to get married, like I'm against men or something! It's been so long since I even had a date that I'm not sure I remember how to act."

Laura squeezed the hand beneath hers. "It's like riding a bike. You never forget."

"Don't be too sure." Katy fingered the unpainted dowel supporting her magic wand. "Makes me sorry this magic wand doesn't really work. I'd sure like to conjure up a fiancé to keep my family off my back and Grandma alive for another year.''

Snatching up the wand, she gave it a sharp crack over her head. It *whapped* into somebody or something, and she froze, afraid to look. Her horrified gaze begged Laura to tell her she hadn't smacked some little old lady.

Laura laughed. ''Hi, Dylan. What are you doing skulking around behind us that way?''

''Dylan!'' Katy twisted in her chair. ''Thank heaven it's only you. I was afraid I'd hurt somebody.'' She waited for him to make some sarcastic remark.

He stood there rubbing his right elbow, one eyebrow cocked while he looked down at the two women with a calculating expression on his face. A local rancher, he wore the uniform of his trade: denim pants, plaid shirt, boots and hat. Many women had raved to Katy about his good looks but she couldn't see it; all she could see was the kid who'd pestered her and tried to get the best of her nearly her entire life.

When he simply continued looking at them with that unfamiliar gleam in his eye, she added, ''That's what you get for sneaking around behind people. What *are* you doing back there?''

''Eavesdropping.'' He said it as if it were a virtue. ''Mind if I join you?'' He plopped down in an empty chair and placed his hat on the table, brim up.

''Yes, I mind,'' Katy said, not expecting him to pay that the slightest attention, which he didn't. ''And you've got some nerve, eavesdropping on a private conversation.''

"Yeah, I do." He gave them both a winsome smile. "I couldn't help but overhear."

"Couldn't *help?* We were hardly shouting."

"Katy," he drawled, "you've got a voice that could shatter glass. I just seem to hear it above any hubbub."

That brought a reluctant smile. "Okay," she said ungraciously, "you eavesdropped. Now I suppose you have some caustic comment to make."

"No." He looked offended. "Look, you need a fiancé in name only. You can't help it if you're a wallflower."

This was the Dylan she knew. "So?" She felt her cheeks grow hot with embarrassment. It was one thing to confide her lack of sex appeal to her best friend but quite another to discover an old adversary had also heard.

"So..." He sucked in a deep breath. "Surprise! So do I."

For a moment she simply stared at him. Then she said, "I beg your pardon? So do you, what?"

"Need a fiancée," he said patiently.

"For what? If this is a joke, Dylan Cole, so help me I'll—"

"It's no joke," he said quickly. "Calm down, Katy. See, since Matt got married I seem to have become the favorite target of every love-starved female in town. Plus, Brandee's back in town."

"Brandee Haycox? Head cheerleader, homecoming

queen, all-around Miss Popularity—*that* Brandee Haycox?''

''Ha-ha,'' he said, ''very funny. There's only one Brandee Haycox.''

''Which has what to do with you? Last I heard, she'd gone off to run a health club in Denver or some such.''

''And now she's healthy and she's moved back again.'' He squirmed in his chair. ''And she...uh...seems determined to add me to her list of conquests, if you know what I mean.'' He gave a self-conscious shrug of wide shoulders. ''My spirit is unwilling but my flesh is weak. I gotta do something to protect myself, fast.''

Laura looked puzzled. ''I don't get it, Dylan. Can't you just tell her you're not interested?''

''I *am* interested—heck, a man would have to be dead not to be—but not in any long-term way, if you get my drift. I need someone to save me from myself.''

''Or save Brandee,'' Katy said, annoyed because it seemed to her that he was trivializing her own problem, which was much more serious—i.e., more important—than his own. ''Good grief, Dylan, you've never been a wimpy sort of guy. Just avoid her— avoid all of them.''

He gritted his teeth. ''It's not a matter of wimpy, it's a matter of survival. And there's something else.'' He looked disgusted. ''Since Brandee's daddy owns just about everything in this town, including the bank that holds my mortgage, I'd just as soon not offend his baby girl.''

Katy nodded emphatically. "Okay, I get it. So your plan is to...what?"

"Well," he said, "before I overheard you moaning and groaning about needing a fiancé, I didn't have a plan. But now it occurs to me that if I wasn't available, Brandee and the rest of 'em might take the hint."

"What happens when she realizes your new love isn't exactly on the up and up?"

He smiled. "You know Brandee. By then, she'll have moved on to someone better."

Katy did, indeed, know Brandee. Which meant she also knew he was right on in his assessment of the beauteous blonde. Brandee didn't have a mean bone in her body but she could be very tunnel-visioned—and she liked men. A lot. "How long do you need this fictional sweetheart?" Katy wanted to know.

"I dunno, not too long. A few months? You?"

"A few months," she agreed. "Until my birthday, for sure."

He nodded. "October twenty-fifth."

She gaped. "You remember my birthday?"

"Why not? I went to enough of your stupid birthday parties growing up." He made a face. "The only thing that made it bearable was that your mother always baked a good cake."

"Yeah, and she's the one who made me invite you. She always liked 'that nice Cole boy.' Which proves she didn't really know you."

Dylan grinned. "Your mom likes me? That's great. I need all the fans I can get." His expression grew cautious. "So what do *you* think?"

"Give me a minute to think about this." Eyeing him warily, she wondered if there was any way they might get along for more than five minutes, even with so much at stake. Certainly he was not bad looking— handsome, according to many. Owner of the Bear Claw Ranch west of town, he was popular with men and sought after by women, one of whom had caught him; he'd been married and divorced.

But could they make such a charade work? Unfortunately, Katy was desperate enough to find out....

"Okay," she said, "we might as well give it a try. What do we have to lose?"

"Yeah," he agreed. "Nothing except our lives."

"We'll have to get a lot of things straight first," she warned. "For example, how will we ever convince anyone we're a couple?"

He grinned. "I've got a tougher question than that. How will we ever convince anyone that a dyed-in-the-wool career woman like you even *wants* to get married?"

"Why, of all the nerve!" She practically sputtered in her outrage. "Of course, I want to get married! What makes you think—"

Laura waved her hands for order. "Hold it, you two. This is no place to work out the details."

Katy glanced around, saw several pairs of eyes watching, and groaned. "You're right. Where—?"

"My house."

Dylan blinked. "*Your* house, Laura?"

She nodded. "For dinner tomorrow night at six—

the kids need to eat early, and then we—I mean *you* can work out all the details without an audience.''

Dylan made a face. ''Matt will really get a kick out of this.''

''Quit grumbling,'' Katy snapped. ''We'll be there, Laura.''

''Speak for yourself,'' Dylan flared.

''Okay, the floor is yours.'' She slumped back in her chair peevishly.

''We'll be there, Laura,'' he said, as if this were new information. ''Now if you ladies will excuse me—'' Lifting his hat from the table and clapping it on his head, he rose and strode toward the door.

Katy stared after him until he'd disappeared outside. Then she groaned. ''Laura, what have I done?''

''Everything you can to make your grandmother happy. Remember that, Katy.''

As if she could forget. There was no other reason in the world she'd deliberately subject herself to the company of Dylan Cole.

Dinner with the Reynolds family was curiously awkward.

Katy couldn't quite figure out why. Matt and Laura were her dearest friends, and she adored their talkative children. And although she didn't put Dylan into those exalted categories, she was, at least, accustomed to him.

Maybe it was just the strain of trying not to fight with him.

Whatever it was, he seemed to be feeling the pressure, too. In fact, he looked entirely ready to grab his hat and run out the door at the slightest provocation.

"So," Matt said, lifting another piece of Laura's good fried chicken off the platter, "what do you two think about the new gasoline station going up on the west side of town?"

"I think it's a crime," Dylan said swiftly, right over Katy's, "I think it's high time!"

They looked at each other across the table, frowning.

Katy said, "If you lived over there, you wouldn't be so quick to condemn. I have to drive halfway across town now to fill up my car."

"And if you had any concern for the environment and runaway growth, you wouldn't mind driving a couple of blocks further," he shot back. "That's what's wrong with people today. All they think about is themselves."

"Why, of all the cotton-headed approaches to urban planning—"

"Not to mention overpopulation. If we don't do something to stop it, Colorado's going to turn into another California. Why, just the other day—"

"*Excuse me.*" Laura gave them a warning glance. "Can you hold off on that until the kids are excused?"

Ten-year-old Jessica, seated beside Katy, grinned. "I don't want to be excused. I think it's fun to hear Aunt Katy and Uncle Dylan fight."

Laura rolled her eyes. "*Fighting* is not fun. How about I give you kids an ice cream bar for dessert and you can eat it outside while the grownups talk?"

"She means 'fight,'" Jessica confided to seven-year-old Zach, who was listening with wide eyes. "Sure, Mom. We know when someone wants to get rid of us."

Once the kids were through the door, Matt chuckled. "When Laura told me what you two are up to, I told her it would never work. Was I right?" He looked lovingly at his wife, who sighed.

Katy felt duty-bound to defend her friend's faith in her. "Look, if Dylan and I want to make it work, it'll work."

The gentleman in question raised his brows. "*Do* we want to make it work?"

She let out her breath on a gust of displeasure. "If you're going to take that attitude...no."

"Katy!" Laura exclaimed. "I thought your mother and grandmother—"

"I'd do it for them if I could, but I don't really see any way." Katy shook her head in disgust.

Laura turned to Dylan. "And what about Brandee Haycox?"

Matt bolted upright in his chair. "Brandee's after you now? Dylan, why didn't you tell me?" He began to laugh.

"I didn't tell you because I knew this would be your reaction." The corners of Dylan's attractive mouth curved down. "And because I knew *you* wouldn't have any tips on how to dislodge her."

"Oops." Matt glanced at his wife. He'd been Brandee's target once himself, before he and Laura got together.

Laura frowned. "I just don't get it," she complained. "You're two of my favorite people and——"

"Since when?" Katy shot a challenging glance at Dylan. "I never thought you liked that guy."

Laura laughed. "I didn't—and I didn't like *this* guy, either." She touched her husband's arm tenderly. "Which all goes to show you that things aren't always what they seem."

Katy rolled her eyes. "Skim milk masquerades as cream," she agreed, "but I've never heard of cream masquerading as skim milk."

Dylan frowned. "Am I being insulted, here? Katy, there's no law saying we have to go out there and make fools of ourselves trying to convince folks we're a couple. If we told them we'd buried the tomahawk, they'd think we buried it in each other's back."

"Absolutely." She nodded for emphasis. "This will never work, so it's good we found out right away. No hard feelings." She offered her hand.

"Naw."

He took her hand in a grip she felt all the way to her shoulder, but she wouldn't allow herself to flinch.

He added, "At least no more hard feelings than usual. Kind of a shame, actually."

She knew she shouldn't ask, but she did anyway. "What's kind of a shame?"

"That a good-lookin' woman like you can't find some guy willing to tame you into something approaching a woman. Because——"

"Out of here!" Laura surged to her feet. "If you two want to go at it hammer and tongs, don't do it in my kitchen!'' She pointed toward the door with a quivering finger.

"Sorry." Dylan jumped up. "We wouldn't want to upset the pregnant lady. Thanks for a great meal, Laura. And thanks for trying."

"Ditto." Katy rose, too. "I'm sorry about all that. Old habits die hard, I guess."

"Maybe, but they *can* die—if either of you really wanted that to happen."

"I suppose. As he said, dinner was great and your intentions were even better." Katy hesitated. "Sure I can't help you with the dishes?"

"You run along." Laura, equilibrium restored, smiled. "And think about how much easier life would be for all of us if you and Dylan could just *get along.*"

"I'll do that," Katy promised, adding a silent *when hell freezes over.*

She kept that state of mind all the way home to her little house on the edge of town. Complete with white picket fence, it was her pride and joy.

The phone was ringing when she unlocked the door. It was her mother, Liz, who lived in Denver with the rest of the Andrewses, including Katy's "little" brothers: Mack, twenty-six, and Josh, twenty-seven; and her grandmother, Edna. Katy's father had died nearly five years ago.

"What's up, Ma?" she asked, tossing her shoulder bag on the sofa. "Everybody all right?"

"Everybody's wonderful," Liz said in her usual upbeat manner. "I've got some good news, Katy."

"I can use some of that."

"We're having a family reunion October fourth. Everybody's coming—Uncle Tom and the kids from Omaha, Aunt Gertrude and her family from Tulsa, all of 'em."

"Sounds great," Katy said cautiously. Not that she didn't love her family, and the big reunions were always fun, but she sensed a hidden minefield here someplace. "I'll bet Grandma's excited."

"Oh, she is! But...there's this little problem...."

"Uh-oh."

Liz's tone changed, became cajoling. "Katy, you know how concerned your grandmother is that you're not married, or even seeing anyone special. And with her health the way it is...well, I know you'll understand."

Katy's heart stood still. "Understand what?"

"Why I've taken the liberty of getting you a date for the reunion, dear. He's a very nice boy, a friend of your brothers', and he's really looking forward to meeting you. He's a lawyer with one of the best firms in town and he—"

"Stop!" Katy's mind raced. A friend of her brothers'? She'd rather die an old maid.

"But Katy, dear, your grandmother..."

"Grandma doesn't have a thing to worry about," Katy lied through her teeth, "because..." Say it! "Because...because I'll have my own date, thank you very much. As a matter of fact, I *have* been seeing someone and—and it's getting serious."

So there!

The negotiating dinner at Laura's had been even worse than Dylan expected and he hadn't expected much. Disgusted, he decided to stop at the Painted Pony Saloon on his way home and have a beer with his buddies, some of whom were sure to be there.

Sure enough, he found a couple of friends holding up one end of the bar and joined them. He got his beer and kept his mouth shut except when he was drinking it.

Until one of the guys leaned over and whispered, "Guess who just walked in, good buddy?"

Dylan knew who it was by the cold chill that shot down his spine. Slowly he turned to find Brandee smiling and waving from the other side of the room, where she stood with a couple of other women he knew—single women eyeing the cowboys at the bar with interest.

He didn't wave her over, but she came just the same, swinging her hips in tight jeans and grinning broadly.

"Hi, sugar." Rising on tiptoe, she planted a firm kiss on his stiff lips. "Fancy meeting you here."

"Yeah. Fancy that."

"Wanna buy me a drink?"

"Love to, but I can't stay to watch you drink it." Draining his glass, he motioned to the bartender. "Bring the lady whatever she wants and then clear my tab," he instructed.

Brandee frowned. "What's the hurry?" she complained. "I hardly ever see you here."

"Well, I just came from—"

"Hang around and you can take me home." She

looped an arm around his waist and squeezed meaningfully.

Dylan felt the breath of doom on the back of his neck. "I'd like to, Brandee, but I can't."

"Why can't you?" Her blue eyes challenged him.

"Uhh…because…ahh…" He thought fast, or rather his thoughts tumbled fast. "Because…I'm taken."

That stopped her, at least momentarily. "Taken?"

"You know, I've got a girl."

"You're kidding!"

"Would I kid you?"

She laughed. "If you thought you could get away with it. Who is this mysterious 'girl' you say you've got?"

He strove to look hurt. "Are you saying you don't believe me?"

She considered, then nodded. "Exactly. I've known you too long to fall for your line. I'll have to see her for myself."

Dylan sucked in a deep breath. His back to the wall, he grasped at straws. "Drop by here Friday night and you'll see her, all right."

And even after you do, he added silently, you may not believe it.

I sure as hell don't.

CHAPTER TWO

KATY PUT THE FINAL POLISH on an advance story for a city planning commission meeting, pushed the "send" button on her computer, and leaned back in her chair with a sigh. Now she'd have time to think about what she'd been putting off since the phone call from her mother last night.

Which was, how to maneuver Dylan into thinking it was his idea to give their "engagement" another shot. Because no way did she want to grovel to get him to give it another try. On the other hand, she couldn't bear to face another of her mother's ill-conceived matchmaking attempts. In the past, she'd been "fixed up with" an aspiring professional wrestler, an accountant, and a college professor.

To say none of these efforts had worked out was an understatement. At least with Dylan, she knew what she'd be getting into. As her father used to say, "The devil you know is better than the devil you don't know."

So how was she going to get Dylan to do her bidding? She called Laura and explained her dilemma.

Laura didn't mince words. "Couldn't you just level with him? I don't see what's wrong with telling the truth."

"Easy for you to say, now that you're married and above the fray," Katy said indignantly. "I've *got* to get him to play along with this but I don't dare give him the upper hand by letting him know how important it is to me. I thought you, of all people, would understand.''

''Why?'' Laura sounded completely unperturbed. ''I've *never* understood why you and Dylan treat each other like enemies. Just because he pulled your hair in third grade doesn't seem sufficiently sinister to keep this feud alive.''

Great, Katy thought, hanging up. Even her best friend didn't understand. Now what was she going to—

''Got a minute?''

She started and looked around to find Dylan standing just behind her desk in the newsroom. She swallowed hard and tried not to look or sound guilty. ''Sure.''

He glanced around somewhat furtively. Katy was the last staff writer to get off deadline so the newsroom was empty except for the sports editor, who looked up with a grin and a wave for the popular Dylan.

''Can we get out of here?'' he asked abruptly.

''Look, I've got a lot to do. I have phone calls out all over the county and—'' She stopped speaking abruptly. After all, *she* wanted something from *him* and this wasn't the way to get it. ''Never mind. You can buy me lunch, if you want.''

''Big whoopee.'' His mouth curved down at the corners unhappily. ''I guess I could do that.''

''If you're short of cash, I could buy *you* lunch.''

She snatched up her shoulder bag from beneath her desk.

"That'll be the day! You think John Wayne let women buy him lunch?"

"Why, you big—!" And then she saw he was laughing at her and she had to laugh herself.

Why was she so darned quick to jump on every word he said? She'd have to watch that if she was going to finagle him into doing her bidding.

Katy dropped the paper napkin on her lap and glanced around the Rawhide Café. "Looks like we're giving the locals plenty to talk about," she said dryly.

"Looks like." Dylan resisted the almost unbearable impulse to fidget. If he was going to get Katy to take another shot at togetherness, however phony, he couldn't let her know it mattered that much to him.

The silence stretched out. "Well?" she finally said impatiently. "I know you've got an ulterior motive for luring me here, so out with it."

He toyed with his fork. "I just…I just wanted to make up for being a grouch last night."

"Dylan, you're always a grouch. This is, however, the first time you've apologized for it."

"Am I?" He frowned.

"You certainly are." She hesitated and the belligerence of her manner softened. "To tell the truth, I guess I'm usually a grouch with you, too. Apparently I just rub you the wrong way."

If she ever rubbed him the right way—he yanked his thoughts up short, wondering what had come over him. This was Katy Andrews, after all, not just any good-lookin' woman. "Then you accept my apology?" His voice sounded uncharacteristically rough.

She considered, her green eyes narrowing. "Sure," she said finally, "why not?"

He felt a load lifting from his shoulders. "Great. Then how about we put our plan in motion by going to happy hour at the Painted Pony Friday night?"

"Going to—you mean, together? Like a date?" Those remarkably long-lashed eyes widened.

"I mean, like we planned. Remember, engagement? Make the grandma happy, scare off my legions of admirers?"

For a moment she stared at him, and then she leaned back in her chair, stifling laughter. "You're suggesting that we reinstate Plan A?"

"Yeah," he said sheepishly, "I guess I am. What do you say, Katy? If we both make a real effort—"

"Burgers and fries, coming up." The skinny kid waiter plunked two overflowing platters before them, and Dylan was forced to wait for her answer through the obligatory checklist: mustard, catsup, mayonnaise, extra pickles and lettuce, toasted bun. The woman made a production out of eating a lousy hamburger!

By the time the waiter withdrew, Dylan had lost any slight degree of patience he might have had. "Well, what's your answer?"

She cut her hamburger in half but he could tell she was still watching him. "This is important to you, isn't it?"

"Hell, no!" He shrugged that suggestion away.

"In that case—"

"*I meant* to say, hell yes." He didn't want to lose her, even if he had to swallow a little pride.

"In that case, my answer is yes." She looked at him with a self-satisfied expression. "But just remember, you wanted this more than I did, so you owe me, Dylan Cole."

"Yeah, and you'll never let me forget it," he muttered, staring down at the huge double burger and crisp steak fries on his plate.

And realizing that he'd mysteriously lost his appetite.

The Painted Pony Saloon was the local hot spot on Friday nights, starting with a happy hour—two drinks for the price of one—from five to seven and then dancing from eight until midnight. Katy had come a few times with dates, more often with girlfriends. It was the kind of place where women could do that without feeling threatened.

As a matter of fact, she'd never felt as threatened then as she did now, walking in on Dylan's arm. They drew so many stares that she felt downright out of place.

"Wanna sit at the bar?" he inquired.

"No, I do *not* want to sit at the bar," she snapped. "How about that table over there by the dance floor?"

"The music will be starting in less than an hour and it gets too noisy down front."

"Is that a crack because I was late and the best tables are already taken? I told you, that last interview ran way longer than it should have."

"Katy," he said in a voice as cold as a well-digger's knees, "if you don't shut up at least until we find a table, I'm going to shut you up myself."

She faced him with hands on her hips. "How are you going to do that? If you lay a hand on me, I'll have you arrested. I'll have you hauled away in chains. So how do you plan to shut me up yourself?"

"I only know one way," he said grimly. "If I grabbed you and kissed you right here in the middle of the Painted Pony, that would shut you up pretty damned fast."

She rocked back on her heels, shocked to the soles of her feet. Kissing Dylan Cole, or being kissed by him, was not something she had ever contemplated...willingly.

Before she could get her battle flags flying again, he took her hand and half-led, half-dragged her to a table in the corner. Once there, he guided her into a chair, then sat himself.

"Okay," he said with a sigh that sounded like relief, "now you can insult me to your heart's content."

He looked so resigned to his fate that she had to laugh. His answering smile was both surprised and strangely warm.

"You win," she said. "I'll *try* to be nice, but with you, that's a real stretch."

"Maybe it'll help if you remember it's for a worthy cause," he suggested. "If we can't even convince folks we're a couple—dating and dancing and the whole nine yards, I don't see how we'll ever convince 'em we're engaged. And if nobody believes us, your grandma won't either."

"Sad but true." She hauled in a deep breath. "Okay, I'm going to pretend that you're Tom Cruise."

"Too short."

"Tom Selleck?"

"Too old."

"Little Tommy Tucker—I don't care! I just need someone to think about so I don't jump down your throat every two seconds."

"You mean, like now?"

Her shoulders slumped. "Exactly like now. Here's a new idea. Why don't we just declare a truce—in public, anyway?"

"Works for me." He glanced at his watch. "It's three minutes of seven. Shall we start on the hour?"

"You got it."

"First person who slips owes the innocent party, big time."

"Absolutely. Seven o'clock."

"In that case—Katy, I hate that thing you're wearing. It looks like an explosion in a fireworks factory."

Offended, she looked down at the bright print of her sundress. "I'll have you know, this dress cost me a lot of money."

"Money can't buy everything."

"No, but it can buy a lot. Speaking of which, don't you own anything except jeans and long-sleeved plaid shirts? I've often wondered if there was something wrong with your arms—flabby, weak, whatever—the way you keep them covered up."

"Wanna find out?" Reaching for the top snap, he

fumbled to open it, his eyes glinting dangerously. "We'll see who—"

"Oops, seven o'clock." She glanced at her watch to confirm this. "As I was saying, I just love a man in a cowboy suit, Dylan darlin'."

He managed the switch in attitudes as seamlessly as she had. "And I love a woman who knows what she loves."

Just then the cocktail waitress dashed up, ending the verbal sparring for the moment. But not before Katy felt a little thrill of dangerous anticipation dart down her spine.

Dylan should have been glad the Pained Pony was filling up so fast, but for some reason, all those people piling in simply added to his tension. It didn't take a genius to know he and Katy were the prime topic of conversation. Although he wasn't a particularly private person, all the attention was getting on his nerves.

So were the inevitable questions he got every minute he was away from her, as in fetching drinks, waiting while she visited the ladies' room, watching her dance with those strong enough to ask.

Yeah, strong, he thought watching her in the arms of Mickey Evans, a fireman. He knew she intimidated most guys and with good reason. A lot of people thought it was her job that made her so willing to ask or say things that others would be too timid to touch, but Dylan knew better.

Katy had always been that way. As a pigtailed kid, she'd run with the boys and held her own with the

best of them—Matt and Dylan not excluded.
Anything they could do, she could do, too.

Or bust bones trying. Like the time she jumped out
of the cottonwood tree when none of the boys would,
because you had to be real careful or real lucky to
avoid the rocks along the creek bank. Katy had been
neither. She'd hit those rocks and broken a leg.

He smiled. She'd taken it like a man and her cast
had been a badge of honor.

The thing was, other girls grew out of that tomboy
stage. Katy hadn't. Even while she changed from gangly hellion into beautiful young woman on the outside, her wild spirit did *not* change.

That was why she and Dylan were still at odds all
these years later. And why most of the guys in town
gave Katy Andrews a wide berth.

"Hi, handsome."

The breathy voice in his ear didn't surprise him;
he'd seen Brandee enter earlier and figured she'd been
waiting for her chance.

She slipped into Katy's vacant chair. "So this is
what I came to see—you and Katy Andrews. Do you
think I was born yesterday, Dylan? It's me—Brandee!
I've known you both *forever*, and the thought of you
two as a couple is hysterical!"

"Katy and I don't think so."

"You mean you actually expect me to believe that
you have a thing going with Katy?"

He liked that: *a thing*. They sure did! "We don't
give a damn what you believe, Brandee," he said. "I
was just trying to make you understand why I'm not
available."

''Sure you are. I mean, here you sit while she dances with that cute fireman. If that's not available, I don't know what is.''

The fast music played by the small band at the edge of the dance floor ended. Mickey and Katy turned back toward the table, and Dylan knew the precise moment she spotted Brandee in her chair. Katy's eyes narrowed and her entire expression grew watchful.

The band started in on a new piece, slow this time. Dylan stood abruptly. ''If you'll excuse me, I'm going to dance with my girl,'' he said to Brandee. If Katy had heard, she wasn't going to be happy but a man had to do what a man had to do.

Taking her into his arms, Dylan swept Katy back onto the dance floor. She followed him effortlessly. In all the years they'd known each other, they'd never danced together, but he'd seen her dance with others enough to know she was good: graceful and intuitive in her movements.

Now she flowed against him with perfect ease. He slid a hand around her waist while the other lifted her hand to press it against his chest. The startled green eyes flew open just before he pulled her closer.

Her voice was muffled. ''Aren't you laying it on a bit thick?''

''Not hardly.'' He led her into a swooping turn, which she followed without faltering. Damn, she felt good in his arms: soft and firm at the same time, warm and fragrant as a summer day.

Too bad it was just Katy.

''Brandee giving you a hard time?'' she asked.

"Trying to. How 'bout we both just shut up and dance?"

"I suppose we could try that."

They did. On the crowded dance floor, they moved closer and closer together——out of pure self-defense, he told himself, tightening his grip. If he hadn't known it was Katy he was dancing with, he could have fooled himself into believing this could be the start of something good.

Funny that they'd never danced together before, though. It wasn't a half-bad experience.

The music stopped. After a moment she said, "You can let me go now."

"Oh, yeah, sure. Sorry."

He couldn't imagine what he'd been thinking of, he conceded, guiding her through the crowd. Maybe just the jolt he'd gotten when she let him hold her so close.

Brandee was waiting. "Hi, Katy," she said. "Dylan tells me you two are a couple. Any truth to that?"

Dylan held his breath.

"I wouldn't exactly say we're a couple." Katy smiled and he relaxed again. "On the other hand, I wouldn't say we aren't, either."

Brandee rolled her eyes. "That's pretty hard to believe for those of us who've been around."

"Oh, you've definitely been around," Katy said. "But things change, Brandee. So tell me, what's the Chamber of Commerce and your father the president doing about paying off the bills they ran up for the Fourth of July celebration?"

"How would I know?" Brandee retorted. "I don't pay any attention to that stuff."

"Well, I *do*. It's part of my job. If—"

Her words were suddenly muffled by Dylan, who clapped a hand firmly over her mouth. "No more shop talk," he announced. "Want another drink?"

She shoved his hand away. "I certainly don't," she said indignantly.

"Want something to eat?"

"I certainly don't."

"Want to go home?"

"Bingo!" She grinned at Brandee. "Going home's not the big attraction. It's saying good night that I enjoy."

And she winked. She actually winked.

Dylan could have kissed her.

"Yuck!" She made spitting noises. "I can't believe I said that—*saying good-night*. I'm ashamed of myself." She glanced at him out of the corner of her eye, thinking he looked mighty smug.

Sounded it, too, when he said, "I thought you did just fine. You can't be subtle with Brandee, in case you didn't know. Not that you're noted for your subtlety or anything."

"Is that a slam?" She stumbled over a broken patch of asphalt and he caught her arm to help her.

"Nah, that was the truth."

They reached his pickup truck and stopped while he fumbled in his jeans pocket for the keys. They'd parked right beneath a street light where it was literally as bright as day.

"Got it." He hauled out the keys triumphantly. "Just let me—damn!"

"What? What is it?"

"Brandee and a bunch of her friends, standing over there in the shadows watching." He spoke in a muted whisper.

"Where?"

"Don't look!" He turned her away, so she was looking in another direction. "Apparently she still doesn't believe us."

Katy shrugged. "Not much we can do about that."

"Yeah, there is."

"Such as? We can't drip water onto her forehead until she's convinced. I don't see—"

"Dammit, Katy, I guess I'd better kiss you." He added hastily, "Of course, it'll be like kissing my sister."

"For sure," she agreed, but her heart leaped crazily in her breast, "and a sister you don't like at that."

"Ready?"

He looked down at her, the light haloing his dark hair, his features completely obscured.

"You mean you weren't kidding?" Her heart pounded a hundred miles an hour.

"Hell, no!"

"But I can't just *kiss* you."

"Why not? It's easy." He put his hands loosely on her shoulders.

She shivered. "B-because I'm not in the habit of kissing just anybody."

"I'm not just anybody, I'm your soon-to-be fiancé."

"Nevertheless, I c-can't put my heart into it without some emotional content."

"Emotional *what?* Look, Katy, we're just talking about a kiss here. A very simple kiss between... between friends...."

He drew her a tiny fraction closer, despite her determination to hold back. He was strong, far stronger than she'd imagined, and she felt herself beginning to lose control of this situation.

"We're not friends," she managed to say. "We're...we're..."

He bent toward her. "What are we, Katy? Can't wait to see what word you come up with."

"We're—" Doomed, she thought, lifting her hands to touch the wide shoulders while his hands drifted to her waist. "We're going to put Brandee's suspicions to rest once and for all, I hope."

"That's the spirit."

His lips touched hers, and it was *not* like kissing her brother. It was like kissing Tom Cruise and Tom Selleck and all the other Toms all rolled into one. With her eyes tightly closed, she felt herself whisked away on a magic carpet to some mythical place where there were no more answers, only questions.

He lifted his head and he was breathing hard. "She's gone," he said in a voice that came out a little husky. "For a woman who doesn't like kissing without emotional content, you're damned good."

Releasing her, he unlocked the cab of the pickup, opened the door and lifted her onto the high seat. This time when he grinned, the lamp illuminated his devilish expression clearly.

"Just for the record," he said, "it was *not* like kissing my sister."

To that, she had no response.

At the newspaper office Monday, Katy was met with smiles by everyone she met, up to and including her boss, John Reynolds, owner, publisher and editor of the Rawhide *Review* and the grandfather of Laura's husband, Matt.

"Hear you got yourself a new beau," he said cheerfully. "That Dylan Cole is a fine man. You could do worse, Katy."

Katy felt her cheeks flame with embarrassed dismay. "What *are* you talking about?" she demanded. "All I did was go to happy hour with the man and you're turning it into a lifetime commit—" She caught herself up short. That was exactly what they wanted everyone in town to believe, she remembered belatedly.

"Don't bite my head off," John said. "All I know is what a little birdie told me."

Yeah, Katy thought, a little birdie named Brandee. John Reynolds had the best network of contacts she'd ever seen. Heaven help her if she tried to put anything over on him.

By lunchtime, she was running scared; everyone she met looked at her with that speculative little gleam in their eyes. Hoping for sanctuary, she called Laura and wrangled an invitation to lunch.

"I don't think I realized what I was letting myself in for with this crazy scheme," Katy complained, reaching for the tuna salad sandwich Laura had placed before her. "This town has the healthiest grapevine I've ever seen or heard tell of."

"You should have known," Laura said serenely, taking her seat. "You remember all the gossip when Matt and I were just starting to get together? I seem to recall someone explaining to me that they *meant* well, so I shouldn't let it bother me."

"Sounded good when I said it," Katy agreed dourly. "But this is happening a lot faster than I ever expected. I thought it would take us at least a few weeks of being seen together before anybody believed us."

"Maybe the sight of the two of you making out in the parking lot at the Painted Pony speeded things up."

Katy's jaw dropped. "We were *not* making out!"

"Hugging, kissing—most people would call that making out."

"Well, it wasn't." Distracted, Katy dropped her sandwich back on the plate, appetite gone.

"What was it, then?" Laura prodded.

"Just two people pretending."

"Pretending." Laura cocked her head, a question on her face. "So how was it?"

"Laura! I'm shocked you'd ask me a question like that." And shocked at the wave of heat in her own cheeks.

"Sorry, I couldn't resist." Laura's smile was devilish. "It's just that you seem to need some sage advice and all I have is curiosity, just like everyone else."

Jessica trotted into the kitchen with her younger

brother at her heels. "What's *sage?*" she asked. "I already know about *advice.*"

"Sage advice," her mother said, "is very wise advice. That's what Aunt Katy needs right now. Unfortunately, I'm all out of it."

Jessica grinned broadly. "I've got some sage advice," she declared. Turning to Katy, she took her hands and peered deep into her eyes, radiating sincerity. "Aunt Katy, when you want sage advice, like, why don't you just wave your magic wand? That's what it's for, to make things right. Right?"

"Right!"

Jessica gave her mother a triumphant glance and trotted on through to the yard. Zach followed without ever having said a word.

Katy looked helplessly at Laura. "Magic wand, right. But if I'm not mistaken, it was that darned magic wand that got me into this mess!"

CHAPTER THREE

"But I don't *want* to have lunch with you Friday," Katy declared. "I'm too busy. I have places to go and people to see. I don't have time. I lack the inclination."

Dylan leaned his hands flat against her desk and waited for her to run out of steam. Then he said, "I don't care about any of that. If we're gonna make this work, we have to be seen together. Friday's the only time I can make it. I have to come in anyway for supplies so I can kill two birds with one stone."

"I'm not particularly fond of being likened to a dead bird," Katy sniffed. "If you think..." Her indignation wound down and she sighed. "Do I have to?"

"Yeah, you have to."

"All right." She gave in ungraciously, punctuating her words with a condemning glance. "What time and where?"

"I'll pick you up at—"

"I'll meet you."

"Noon at the Rawhide Café."

"That should guarantee an audience, all right. Okay, I'll be there."

"Great."

"You don't have to get sarcastic."

"Maybe I do." For a moment he looked down at

her with a slight frown. Then he straightened and walked out of the room without another word or even a glance.

Katy gritted her teeth in annoyance, but she didn't have time to ponder. She had a story to write, a story questioning expenditures by the Rawhide Chamber of Commerce.

This turned out to be harder to do than she'd expected. Sure, the story was going to tick off chamber officers and members alike but as a reporter, it was Katy's job to print the truth and raise hell without fear or prejudice. No, something else was on her mind, making it hard to concentrate....

Seeing Dylan so early in the day really messed with her mind. That kiss in the parking lot had proven impossible to forget. Over and over again she reminded herself that it was only *Dylan*. But she didn't seem able to talk herself out of the thrill she'd felt when he took her into his arms and pressed his lips to hers....

"Katy!" John stood before her desk, his thick white hair sticking out in all directions and a frown on his round face. "Am I going to get that story or do I have to find something else to fill the hole on the front page?"

"Sorry." She pulled her thoughts up short and hunched dutifully over her computer screen. "I'm hard at work, see?" And she was—hard at work trying to forget the unthinkable.

Dylan rode the big bay gelding up to the corral behind the Bear Claw ranch house and stepped down out of

the saddle. A big black Mercedes was parked in front
and he wondered who'd come to visit.

Whoever it was could wait while he took care of
his horse. Quickly he stripped off saddle and bridle
before reaching for a currycomb. When he heard footsteps, he glanced over his shoulder without pausing
in the long, precise strokes, then did a double take.

Brandee Haycox's father, Edgar. Now what?

"Edgar," he said in greeting.

"Cole."

The man's face was even more florid than usual.
Dylan led the horse to the gate of the corral and
turned him loose. "What brings you to my neck of
the woods?" he inquired, knowing he wouldn't like
the answer.

"This!" Edgar waved a newspaper through the air
with angry swipes. "That woman has gone too far!"

Dylan suppressed a groan. "What woman?" Like
he didn't know.

"That *Andrews* woman, who else? Always out
muck-raking and rabble-rousing. She's got to be
stopped!"

Dylan wasn't too crazy about the way this conversation was shaping up. "I don't see how you can fault
her for raking muck if it's there for the raking," he
said reasonably. "I also don't see why you're telling
me all this. Shouldn't you talk to her, or to her editor?"

"John won't listen to a word against her," Edgar
grumbled. "And when I try to talk to her, she just
starts writing down every word I say and egging me
on to say more."

Dylan stifled a smile. He'd seen Katy do that: deflect angry criticism by offering—some called it *threatening*—to quote the speaker verbatim. The easiest way to hang a man, she once said, was to do it with his own words exactly as he said them.

But he wanted to sooth Edgar Haycox, not stir him up even more. "That still doesn't explain why you came here to shout at me," he said reasonably. "Why don't we go inside and I'll make a pot of coffee. Then maybe we can talk."

"No time," Edgar said impatiently. "As to why I'm here—well, the whole town knows you're dating that—that *journalist*."

"That hardly makes me her keeper."

"No, but it implies some influence." Edgar's fleshy face set into grim lines. "Tell her to back off, Cole. We know we've got...a slight problem with chamber finances, but we've got a committee working night and day to set things right."

"Is that so?" Dylan tried to curb his irritation. "So you're telling me that she got the story right."

"I didn't say that!" the banker blustered.

"You implied it. *She got the story right* but you and the good old boys at the chamber are working to correct the situation and you'd like to avoid further bad publicity while you do it. Have I got it straight?"

Edgar squirmed. "Just between you and me and the gatepost—yes."

Dylan mulled over his options. He didn't need this. He especially didn't need to offend the man who held the mortgage on the ranch.

But he also didn't want to have to justify to himself

why he'd left Katy dangling in the breeze when she was obviously in the right.

Finally he said, "The lady has a mind of her own and she knows how to take care of herself." Understatement if ever there was one. "I'm not your messenger boy. Whatever you have to say, say it to her."

The banker sneered. "You disappoint me. I guess it's clear who wears the pants in that relationship."

Dylan counted to ten—then to twenty. "Edgar," he said, slowly and deliberately, "if you think that's an insult, think again. Katy Andrews is a match for any man, including me. But I'd advise you not to run around town bad-mouthing her, because if you do, I might just have to take action."

Edgar took a startled step back. "Are you threatening violence?"

"Hell, no! I'm promising retribution." Dylan, in control again, winked.

"Drop by any time, but leave the newspaper at home."

"I—why you—don't think—" Edgar sputtered a bit longer, threw the newspaper on the ground, turned and stalked away to the big black car.

Dylan called after him. "My best to Brandee."

That drew no response whatsoever. Before the dust settled in the lane, Dylan snatched up the paper and began to read.

When Katy got home from work that day, Dylan was sitting outside her house in his red truck, obviously waiting. Before she could get the key into the lock, he'd trotted up to the door.

She glanced at him over her shoulder as she opened the front door. "This is a surprise," she said. "I didn't expect to see you until lunch, Friday."

"Yeah, me, too." He followed her inside.

She tossed her shoulder bag and clipboard onto a chair on her way through to the kitchen. Somehow she couldn't shake the uneasy feeling stealing over her. "So what's up?"

"Why don't you tell me?"

"I don't have the time or interest to play games," she snapped, opening the refrigerator. "Want a soft drink?"

"Got a beer?"

"Sure." She pulled out a can of beer and tossed it to him; he caught it one-handed and ripped off the tab. She took out a can of pop for herself and faced him. "What's this all about?"

"I had an unexpected visitor at the ranch a few hours ago."

"Anyone I know?" she asked in a bored tone, her pulse rate already rising.

"Edgar Haycox."

"Uh-oh. Is he mad because you haven't been paying enough attention to his little girl?"

"Nope, he's mad because he claims my *current* girl is smearing his name and that of the Rawhide Chamber of Commerce all over the front page of the Rawhide *Review*."

"Oh, my goodness!" She stared at him. "He actually said that?"

"About smearing his name?"

"No, about me being your current girl."

He made an exclamation of disgust. "Is that all you got out of what I just said?"

She shook off the funny feeling at being labeled his current girlfriend. "You can't expect me to get too excited because somebody doesn't like something I wrote. It happens all the time when a reporter does the job right. It's not my business to promote the chamber or the town. It's—"

"I know, your business is to print the news without fear or favoritism. Only Edgar calls it rabble-rousing and muck-raking."

She let out an astonished peal of laughter. "You're kidding! Well, I guess I couldn't rake muck if there wasn't any to rake."

"Funny, that's what I told him."

"You defended me?" That unexpected possibility softened her voice...and her heart.

"What else could I do when you were right?" He sounded completely exasperated.

She softened even more. "You mean you believe me?"

"I believed Edgar. He as much as said you had it right, he just thought you should have kept it to yourself and let the chamber clean its own house."

So much for warm and fuzzy feelings. She snapped open her can of soda. "So you drove all the way in to tell me something I already knew—the chamber's on my case."

His strong jaw tightened. "I thought you'd want to

know. *I'd* want to know if somebody was gunning for me.''

"I can take care of myself."

"I told him that, too."

"Then why are you here?" She faced him with her hands on her hips. "You obviously handled everything yourself."

For a moment, he just looked at her, his face expressionless. "I guess I wanted a little credit," he said finally. "I also wanted to suggest to you that it might be a good idea to lighten up on the chamber and give them the chance Edgar asked for—time to do a little house-keeping on their own."

She stared at him. "You want me to back off?"

"Would that mean the end of the world? It's not the same as asking you to throw a ball game."

"It is to me."

"In that case, you just charge in there and let the bodies fall where they may," he shot back at her. "A little caution might be in order, that's all I meant to suggest. But you do what you want. You always do." He headed for the door.

She followed. "You have no right to ask me that. Edgar Haycox—" She grabbed his elbow and he stopped short. "—holds the mortgage on your ranch."

"So?" His hard gaze challenged her.

"So you got into this phony love affair because you didn't want to make the man angry."

"That's right."

"You don't think that casts doubt on your motive for coming here and telling me this?"

His expression grew hard. "That's a hell of thing to say to me. Forget it—I'm sorry I wasted your time." Yanking his arm free, he spun around—and when his foot came down on the floor it was with a sharp crack.

Alarmed, Katy stared down at the remains of her cherished magic wand, made for her by the Reynolds children. "My wand!" She dropped to her knees.

He withdrew his foot hastily. "What the—?"

Katy picked up the shattered dowel. The paper-plate star dangled from the other end. "You ruined it!" she accused, astonished to realize her eyes were growing damp.

"I ruined what? All I see is—what *is* that?"

"Like you don't know!" She whacked at his boot with the remains and the star fell off entirely. "Jessica and Zach made this magic wand. It helped bring Laura and Matt together."

He stared at her. "Katy," he said finally, "I think you've completely lost your marbles this time. I'm sorry I broke that old dowel and stepped on that old paper plate but life is full of travail. All I can say is, get over it!"

"You rat! First you come in here and try to get me to trample on my principles, slant the news—"

"I did no such thing. I tried to get you to be reasonable."

"Now you've broken my magic wand and you don't even care!"

"I care," he said grimly, "but I don't consider it a hanging offense in these parts."

"Get out," she yelled at him. "You're fired as my potential fiancé."

"You can't fire me," he yelled back, "I quit!"

He stomped out. Only after he'd gone did it sink in that he'd actually defended her to Edgar Haycox.

The next day, Katy went in to talk to John as soon as she returned from her rounds. Her editor looked around from his computer with a smile.

"What can I do you for?" he asked.

"There's something I need to talk to you about." Something she'd spent hours thinking about, as a matter of fact.

"I'm all yours." John indicated the chair next to his desk.

She sat. "It's about the story I did yesterday on the Chamber of Commerce."

"You did a good job on that, Katy." His smile was warmly approving.

"Thanks, John. It means a lot to me to hear you say that." She chewed on her lip. "I'm completely confident of my facts."

"Yes." He frowned. "Are you getting a hard time over it?"

She shrugged. "No more than I expected. It comes with the territory."

"Then what's bothering you?"

"I'd like to hold off on a follow-up until they have a chance to get their affairs in order," she blurted. "I don't think there's anything deliberate going on over there. How does that go, about treachery and incompetence? There's some incompetence, sure, but I don't see any treachery.''

He said nothing, just looked at her with a perplexed expression. She wanted to squirm before that level gaze; she'd never asked him anything remotely like this before. Up until now, she'd always been the one pressing to go further and faster.

Now she was saying she wanted to back off. What had happened to her? John, a man whose editorial instincts she trusted completely, was disappointed in her and it was all Dylan's fault! She wanted to hang her head in shame.

"Katy," John said, "I'm proud of you."

That took her breath away. "You are?"

"You've always had the right instincts as a reporter, but I've occasionally wondered if you had the heart. Now I know you do."

She slumped in the chair. "You're kidding."

He shook his head. "I'm not. I'm applauding you." He turned back to his video display terminal. "I'll expect the next chamber story when there's something to report—either they've cleaned up their act or they've proven themselves to be deadbeats. And I'll let you tell me which it is."

She walked out of her editor's office in a daze. Apparently she'd done something right, even if for the wrong reason.

And that reason was…to please Dylan Cole. Too bad it came too late to do any good.

Dylan came into town Thursday instead of Friday for supplies because he didn't intend to keep the lunch date with Katy, and he didn't want to deal with avoiding her. Standing in the loading dock of the Rawhide Feed and Seed, he was almost relieved to see that the woman approaching him was Brandee, not Katy.

She gave him a smile. "Hi, Dylan. Where you been keeping yourself?"

He shrugged vaguely. "I've...been around."

"But not much. The way I hear it, you've been hiding out at that ranch of yours."

"Yeah, well..." He edged toward his pickup truck.

She edged right along with him. "I hear you and Katy are kaput."

"Where'd you hear that?" It kind of annoyed him that the gossips were already at work.

"Around. I guess she doesn't see the handwriting on the wall where you're concerned, though."

Dylan's ears perked up. "What does that mean?"

"Well, after she pulled back on the chamber story, I'm sure she thought that you'd come running."

"She did *what?*"

"Pulled back on the chamber story. She told Daddy that she was going to give them a chance to take care of the problems themselves. If they did, she'd write about that. If they didn't, she'd write about that, too."

"Good for her," he said softly.

Brandee frowned. "Naturally, after you went to her on Daddy's behalf—"

"I did *what?*"

She looked defensive. "You did, didn't you? Daddy said he talked to you and you got kind of hostile. But obviously you talked to her. It's also obvious that she only pulled back because you asked her to—I mean, has anyone ever heard of Katy Andrews backing off on *anything?*"

As a matter of fact, he never had. But could she possibly have done it because he asked her to? That possibility, however remote, stunned him. To the waiting Brandee, he said, "Katy does what she thinks is right. It has nothing to do with me."

"Yeah, sure." She shrugged it off, stepping closer with a smile. "Now that you're available, I thought maybe you and I might pick up where we left off."

He saw an abyss opening beneath his feet. "We might, but I'm *not* available." He opened the pickup door and sprang inside.

"But—"

"Didn't you ever hear of a lover's quarrel? That's all it was."

He drove away, thinking that he'd overreacted, thinking that Katy had overreacted, thinking that she'd gone way out on a limb for him and never even told him about it.

Thinking that he probably didn't have much chance of reinstating their "romance" but that he'd have to give it a try.

Katy came home Thursday night to five telephone messages. One was from someone angry because their newspaper was delivered late; two were "hot tips" on news items; one was from her mother; and the last was from Laura.

She dialed her mother first.

"Oh, hi, honey!" Liz sounded as boundlessly

perky as ever. "I was just calling to update you on the family reunion. It's right around the corner now."

"About that..."

"Yes, everyone's coming and we're all so excited. Especially Mother. When I told her you have a boyfriend—"

"A woman my age doesn't have *boy*friends. That's for kids."

"Whatever. To her, he's a gentleman caller. He *is* a gentleman, isn't he, Katy?"

Was Dylan a gentleman? "I guess you could call him that, only now there's a prob—"

"Don't you tell me there's a problem!" Liz sounded agitated. "I swear, I think it would kill your grandmother if you showed up alone."

"But—"

"And you, Katy—you'd never live it down. Everybody knows."

"Oh, Mother!" Katy groaned. "Did you have to tell the entire world?"

"Certainly not. I told your grandmother and *she* told the world." Liz's laughter still had an edge to it. "We've all been so worried about you, sweetheart— you know, because we were beginning to wonder if you'd ever find a man who could measure up."

"Mother—"

"And your brothers! They can't wait to look this guy over and decide if he's good enough for you. I just hope whoever you're bringing is really special because you know how the boys feel about their big sister."

She certainly did. "The boys," as their mother

called the six-foot-plus brothers, once actually threatened to punch out a date who'd made an unwelcome
pass at their sister.

Liz's tone turned cajoling. "You haven't told me
anything about this guy, Katy, not even if it's someone we know."

"I want you to be surprised," Katy said lamely.
"Only now...well, there's a problem and..."

"Katy Andrews, if you don't show up with a man
on your arm, your grandmother will probably have a
stroke right on the spot."

"That's not fair! You can't expect me to—" But
they could, Katy knew they could. If they thought it
would speed the nuptials, her brothers would probably
go to the mall and kidnap a likely looking stranger.

"You're right," Liz said in a cool voice totally
unlike her own, "it's not fair of me. I apologize."

That was even worse than being manipulated.
"You don't have to apologize."

"No, I *do* apologize. And if you're too busy to
make our simple little reunion, that's all right, too.
I'll tell your grandmother...somehow."

"Mother, stop that. I said I'd come and I will.
And—" Heaven help her; she crossed her fingers.
"I'll bring my fella along with me."

If I have to hold a gun to his head, she promised
herself, hanging up.

So how was she going to get herself out of *this*
pickle?

On Friday, Katy met Laura for lunch at the Rawhide
Café at eleven-forty-five. Arriving a few minutes late,

she made her way across the crowded restaurant and slipped into a chair with a sigh.

Laura, looking as fresh and pretty as a rose, smiled. The nearer she drew to her due date, the more serene she seemed to become. "You look frazzled," she said kindly. "Anything I can do to help?"

"Come back to work?" Katy looked pointedly at the expanding waistline and grimaced. "I guess the answer to that is no, but we sure do miss you. Elsa's trying but she doesn't have a clue what she's doing. I give her a hand when I can find the time, but things have really been hectic this week."

"I can imagine, with that chamber story breaking and all."

Katy sighed. "About that—" The waitress appeared to take their order; then Katy continued. "I asked John if I could hold off on a follow-up on the chamber story until we see how they handle it. He thought that was a good idea, but I'm not so sure."

Laura cocked her head. "If you're not sure, why did you suggest it?"

"Because…" Katy couldn't bring herself to tell the truth; that she did it for Dylan. "It just seemed like a good idea at the time," she said lamely.

Laura nodded. "I'm sure it was—and is. Don't worry about it, Katy. John has many years' experience and he knows this town like the back of his hand. If it wasn't right, he wouldn't have let you do it—period."

"Thanks." Katy smiled. "I needed that." She placed her paper napkin in her lap. "So how's the mama-to-be?"

"Big as a barn and getting really impatient," Laura reported cheerfully. "For some reason, though, I think this baby is going to be early."

Katy shook her head in amazement. "Now how would you know that?"

"I don't *know* it, I just have a feeling." Laura unfolded her napkin. "Like I have a feeling that work's not the only thing that's got you in such a state."

"I'm not 'in such a state,' as you put it."

"Oh, yes you are. And I think it's because things aren't going the way you thought they would with Dylan."

"Now that you mention it…" Katy stared down at her silverware. "Our bargain is off, in case you hadn't heard."

"I heard."

Katy's head snapped up again. "Who told you? I know there's gossip but—"

"Matt told me, and Dylan told him. Relax, will you? You're jumpy as a cat."

"Dylan talks to Matt about me—about us?"

"Why not? You talk to me about Dylan."

"That's different. You're my best friend. If I can't talk to you, I can't talk to anyone."

"Exactly. And as you are well aware, Matt and Dylan have been friends much longer than we have."

"But then Matt tells you. Do you tell Matt what *I* say?"

"Sometimes. But usually he doesn't want to hear—'you women,' he says. 'You turn everything into a global crisis.'"

Katy rolled her eyes. "I don't know whether to be

glad or insulted that he has such a poor opinion of us.''

''Trust me—be glad.'' Laura patted Katy's arm. ''Now tell me what's got you so down in the dumps.''

''My mother called last night, and she is really leaning on me about this family reunion. In a moment of pure panic, I told her I'd be there with my significant other. Only, the man playing the part has bolted.''

''Over what?''

Katy considered how best to answer that. Honesty seemed the best policy. ''I'm not sure,'' she said finally. ''Maybe it was just a misunderstanding. I know he came by to see me with the best of intentions, but one thing led to another and first thing I knew we were yelling at each other. Then when he turned to leave, he stepped on my magic wand and busted it all to smithereens.''

She felt her mouth tremble and pressed her lips together for a moment before going on. ''I can forgive a lot but I'm not sure I can forgive a man who'd break a person's magic wand and then just try to shrug it off.''

''Guys don't understand about stuff like that,'' Laura said.

''They should,'' Katy flared. ''Every time I think about it, I just want to give Dylan Cole a piece of my mind!''

''That's good,'' Laura said approvingly, ''because you're about to get your chance.'' She smiled broadly, focusing above Katy's head. ''Hi, Dylan. Care to join us for lunch?''

CHAPTER FOUR

DYLAN STOOD THERE in the middle of the Rawhide
Café, twisting his hat between his hands and feeling
nervous as a cat in a roomful of rocking chairs. After
the way they'd parted, how could he imagine Katy
would ever take him back?

"Hi, Laura," he said, adding more cautiously, "Hi,
Katy."

Katy twisted around in her chair to glare up at him.
"What are *you* doing here?" she demanded.

"We had a date, remember?"

"Did you think after you stomped all over my
magic wand that I'd ever break bread with you again?
Really, Dylan!"

He frowned, trying to get it all straight. "You saying that you're mad at me over that stupid piece of
paper and wood, but *not* over—?"

"Don't go on!" She glanced quickly around. "We
don't need to air our—I mean, this is a public place."

"You bet your boots, it is." Feeling more confident, he pulled out a chair. Obviously, she didn't want
to create a scene and he was perfectly willing to take
advantage of that weakness.

The waitress arrived with their food: a Caesar salad
for Laura and a huge slab of chicken-fried steak on a
bun with a massive serving of French fries for Katy.
"What can I get for you, Dylan?" she inquired.

"A great big glass of iced tea and a piece of that cherry pie over there in the pie safe."

"That's all?"

"Katy's gonna share," he predicted.

"What gives you *that* idea?" Katy flared, reaching for the catsup bottle.

"The size of that platter. I don't believe there's a woman in town who could eat all that."

Her green eyes flashed. "We'll just see about that." She hesitated, frowned, added to the waitress, "He's right. I knew when I ordered that I couldn't eat it all. Could you bring us another plate, please?"

"Glad to." She walked away laughing.

Laura had watched the exchange with a smile on her face. Now she reached for her fork. "I'm happy to see you two getting along so well," she said very tongue-in-cheek.

"Yeah, well..." Katy sawed the big sandwich in half with her table knife and picked up the smaller portion. She looked at the extra plate set before her by the waitress, then at Dylan. With a sigh, she put the smaller piece on the extra plate, added a few French-fried potatoes and shoved the platter at Dylan.

"Ah, shucks," he made a great issue of demurring, "I didn't mean to leave you short." But he didn't hesitate to pop a fry into his mouth.

"I'm trying to butter you up," Katy said darkly.

She was the only woman he'd ever known whose tone and manner could scold while asking for a favor. "That sounds promising," he said. "As a matter of fact, I have a favor to ask of you, too. Maybe we can make a deal here."

She let out her breath in an exasperated rush. "I certainly hope so, because I'm in a real serious bind. My mother and grandmother expect me to show up at the family reunion a week from next Saturday with the man of my dreams on my arm. I realize arriving with *you* would be stretching the point, but I'm desperate."

"You wanna play 'can you top this?' Brandee dropped by the ranch the other day and—" He stopped short. He didn't want to tell Katy he knew of her conversation with Banker Haycox; that was her secret to tell, if and when she wanted. He skipped straight to the second part of Brandee's visit. "Suffice it to say, she's still on the prowl. So I was hoping we could get back together again...uh, just for a little while...."

They looked at each other and suddenly the air seemed to buzz with electricity. Laura broke the contact.

"There," she said with satisfaction. "Thank heaven that's settled."

Dylan uttered a low "amen," but still he thought Katy might have heard him.

They drove down the mountain to Denver for the reunion in Katy's Jeep Cherokee. She'd insisted; after all, this was *her* family and *her* emergency.

Unlike some men she could name, Dylan seemed to have no problem with a woman in the driver's seat. When he caught her looking at him, he grinned.

"They don't know it's me coming, do they?"

"Nope. I told them I wanted to surprise them."

"This will, guaranteed. How old are your brothers now? Last time I saw them they couldn't have been more than...oh, early teens."

"Mack's twenty-six and manages a sporting-goods store in one of the malls. Josh is twenty-seven and is a personal trainer at a health club, when he isn't out climbing mountains and swimming oceans."

"Yeah, I remember that about them. They were a couple of jocks, all right."

"Uhhh...I'd be a little leery of them if I was you."

His brows rose. "How so?"

"They tend to get a little protective of their only sister, which is one of the reasons I didn't move down the mountain when the rest of the family pulled up stakes in Rawhide. Between them and my mom and grandmother, I never get a moment's peace when I'm around home."

"Because...?"

"Dylan, pay attention!" She shot him a baleful glance. "They want me married, preferably with a dozen kids."

"A dozen may be a tad too many, but I wouldn't mind a few if they were anything like Jessica and Zach."

Her tension evaporated. "They're great kids, aren't they? But they belong to Matt and Laura, and no amount of wishing by my family is going to get me married and pregnant any quicker."

"I don't know," he said mischievously. "It almost got you engaged."

That drew a reluctant grin. "Very funny. Just be

cool, okay? Don't give the boys, as Mother calls them, any reason to get testy.''

''I can handle myself.''

''Yes, but can you handle *them?* I don't want anything to upset Grandma's day.''

''I get the picture,'' he said confidently. He banged his fists on his chest. ''I'm a man's man! I'll have them eating out of my hand in no time.''

Sure he would. Katy drove on, filled with foreboding.

''Katy, Dylan has the boys eating out of his hand.'' Liz Reynolds shook her head in disbelief. ''I'm dumbfounded.''

''So am I, Mom.''

And she was. That rat Dylan had laid on so much charm that he had her entire *family* eating out of his hand. All except her, of course. She knew it was all an act.

Liz smiled. ''I think Grandma has a crush on him,'' she confided. ''I think if he was fifty years older or she was fifty years younger—look out, Katy!''

Katy laughed dutifully, despite the awful thought that had just occurred to her: maybe it was worse to have the whole family in love with Dylan than to have them disappointed in him—and in her. *Now* how was she going to let them all down easy when the time came?

Mack came rushing into the kitchen, sweat gleaming on his bare torso when he extended a flaccid-looking football. ''Quick, Ma, where's the tire pump? This football has lost all its air.''

"The pump is in the garage."

"No, it isn't. I looked there."

"Behind the snow tires in the corner?"

"Oh. I didn't think of that." Mack turned away, then wheeled back. "Katy, you've done all right for yourself this time. That Dylan is aces." He gave her a thumb's up.

Katy gaped at her brother. "I can't believe this is coming from you, of all people."

"Hey, we waited a long time for you to pick out a soul-mate. We know a good one when we see one. But who'd have thought you and ol' Dylan would ever get together? It's a miracle!" He winked and dashed out into the sunshine again.

Katy looked at her mother, despair flooding through her. "This is too much," she said. "I'm beginning to think you guys like him more than you like me."

"Don't be ridiculous." Liz gave her daughter a quick hug. "We like him so much because he makes you happy, and *you* we love." Stepping back, she reached for the pitcher of lemonade on the counter. "Can you take this out and pass it around, dear? I'll be along in a few minutes with the coffee and cookies."

"How anyone can drink coffee on a day this hot is beyond me."

"Trust me, we can. Now run along."

She shooed her daughter outside, pitcher in hand. Katy hesitated on the back step, her gaze automatically searching for Dylan. He wasn't at the picnic table with the aunts and uncles, or under the shade trees with Grandma and Aunt Gertrude. Following their gazes, she saw a pack of kids and adults tossing around the football resurrected by Mack.

A golden god shot up from their midst, reaching high for the football. Katy caught her breath. Like the other guys, Dylan had removed his shirt and was clad only in jeans and sports shoes.

Unlike the other guys, he stood out as if in a spotlight, every chiseled muscle distinct and memorable.

Mouth suddenly dry, she forced herself to turn away. This was getting to be a very sticky wicket indeed....

"Do you *have* to go?"

Katy leaned over and kissed the wizened cheek. "Yes, Grandma, we really have to go." Actually, she'd been gratified to discover that Grandma looked a lot better than Mother had led her to expect.

Dylan also kissed the old lady, sending Grandma into gales of giggles. "I don't have a grandma," he said. "Can I adopt you?"

"Silly boy!" She tapped him lightly and flirtatiously on the chest. "Once you children are married, I'll be your grandma whether you want me or not."

Katy could see how that comment startled him, but doubted anyone else would.

"That's right." He beamed at the old lady. "I can hardly wait."

"That's what's wrong with you young people today. You don't think you *have* to wait." She cocked her head impishly, strands of fine white hair wisping around her cheek. "Which brings up another little item."

Liz slid an arm around her mother's waist. "Mom, I don't think the kids want to—"

"Oh, they don't mind."

Katy was perplexed. "What is it you're getting at, Grandma?"

"Why, children, of course. How many do you fine young people plan to have, and when are you getting started?"

Katy's stomach clenched, and she felt as if all the blood must be draining from her face. "I—why we— really, you can't just—"

Dylan laughed. "Fewer than a dozen," he said. "Just a little while ago on the way here, Katy said twelve was definitely too many."

"Now wait a minute!" Katy tried to reclaim their attention. "We were just—"

"She's right there," Grandma said quickly. "When are you going to march this girl down the aisle and get started?"

"We're not even engaged!" Katy wailed.

"But you will be. I'll be the happiest grandma in Colorado when that happens."

"I know, but—"

"I'd like to hurry things along," Grandma announced. "I don't have all that much time left."

Katy's heart constricted into a lump of foreboding. "Please don't say that."

"Why not? The truth doesn't scare me, just the thought of missing out on your big day. So are you bringing this boy home for your birthday?"

"I can't possibly get away for that myself. I'm really busy at work, and Laura's baby is due about that time, and—"

"—I'm busy, too." Dylan shot her a warning glance.

Grandma waved her hands for attention. "Then I'll go *there*," she announced. "You've been inviting me to come visit and I think your birthday is the perfect time to do it. While I'm there, I can encourage this young man to make it legal."

"There's nothing to make legal." Katy glanced at Dylan for support and instead saw a man enjoying the show.

"Banana oil!" Grandma looked devilish. "I know how you young people are. Don't tell *me* you still haven't—"

"Mother!" Liz looked absolutely horrified.

"You can come, too, Lizzy. We'll have a ball."

Liz rolled her eyes. "My own mother! I can't believe this."

"If you won't come, one of the boys will drive me."

Mack waved his hand. "I'll do it. Dylan invited me to come look over his place."

"Well," Liz mused, "maybe I *could* get away."

"I've been meaning to take a few days off myself," Josh joined in. "I wouldn't mind spending them with my favorite sister. You got room to put us all up, Katy-did?"

"No!"

Dylan said, "I've got plenty of room for—"

"Yes!"

"Which is it, Katy, yes or no?"

"It's yes," she said with a sigh. "Okay, you're all coming up for my birthday, is that right? You do know I'll have to work."

"Your birthday falls on a Sunday this year," Liz said.

"Oh, that's right. Okay." Katy gave in completely, "I'll put you all up and we'll have a birthday party and then you'll all go home." And let me try to find some way out of this mess.

"Sounds like a plan." Mack gave Dylan a high-five. "Yo, big fella!"

"I'm really sorry about that," Katy said, steering the car onto the ramp to the highway heading west into the mountains. "But I did warn you that they have marriage on the brain—at least *my* marriage. Nobody seems to care that the boys are still playing the field."

"Yeah," he agreed. "It's different for women."

She shot him an annoyed glance and found him smiling and obviously waiting for her to react. She gave him a sheepish grin. "You were a good sport. I guess I owe you thanks for that."

"T'weren't nothin', ma'am," he said modestly, going into his good-old-cowboy routine. "To tell you the truth, I always liked your family, especially your grandma."

"I appreciate your saying that, true or not."

His aw-shucks demeanor fell away. "I *do* like your grandma. I wish I had one of my own, but mine died when I was just a kid." He frowned. "Katy, why is it that you never believe anything I say?"

"Habit, I guess. Why is it you say so many things you know are going to set me off?"

He shrugged. "Habit, I guess. That and the fact that you look so cute when you're mad."

"I'll bet you stole that line from some old movie."

"Yeah, I did, but it's still true. I guess I just enjoy a good fight, when it's an even match."

"Why Dylan Cole, you mean ol' *thang,*" she cooed with her best Scarlett O'Hara accent. "Pickin' on poor little ol' me."

He laughed. "That's one of the things I actually like about you," he said. "You can take care of yourself no matter what the boys think."

"Yeah, I can. Political reporting, even in a small town, is not for the faint of heart." She glanced at him, lounging against the passenger door, completely relaxed. This was as good a time as any to ask a question that had nagged at her for years. "Uhh...if you don't mind a nosy question...what caused your marriage to break up? To all outward appearances, you and Shawna were a perfect match."

"You'd have thought so." He didn't look offended, just thoughtful. "She was just too damned perfect for me, Katy. I couldn't live up to her and she couldn't live down to me. Eventually we both got fed up trying." He shot her an amused glance. "This may shock you, but I'm not as easy to live with as you probably think I am."

"I've never given living with you a single thought," she said airily, thinking that now he'd brought it up she just *might.* "At least you're not bitter."

"Not really. I never had a lot of illusions to begin with. I've always thought marriage was just something cooked up by women to keep men in line anyway. But I'm beginning to rethink that position. Now that I'm getting older..."

"Hey, age is certainly better than the alternative."

"Yeah, and there's another plus. Because now that I'm getting older, as I said, I think I might actually work up the guts to try that marriage thing again some day. I figure I'd be a little better at it the second time around." He chuckled. "Not as good as Matt, of course. I...kinda envy him—until I see the things that wife of his gets him to do."

"Like going into the delivery room with her when his child is born?"

"Exactly like that," Dylan said fervently.

"If he loves her, what's the big deal?"

"He loves her, all right. Me? I'd have to worship the ground she walks on to do that."

"It could happen."

"Yeah, and I could be the first cowboy on the moon, but it ain't likely." He gave her a long, level look. "Since we're being so painfully honest, how about you?"

"How about me what?" But she was pretty sure she knew.

"You were engaged a few years back—and then all of a sudden, you weren't. What happened?"

"I made a horrible discovery just in the nick of time."

"Yeah?" He looked interested. "What? He was dishonest, did drugs, drank too much?"

"Nothing like that. I just realized I didn't love him. I *liked* him, but that wasn't nearly enough. So I called it off and he left town—I did feel bad about chasing him out of town. The thing is, I won't get married unless I'm head over heels in love."

"Why, Miss Katy Andrews, you're a romantic. You probably actually believe in all that happily-ever-after stuff."

A smile tugged at her lips. "Don't spread it around, will you? I have my reputation as a tough-as-nails newswoman to protect."

"Your secret's safe with me."

What else was safe with him besides secrets? she wondered as she drove on toward Rawhide. Was *she?* If she pulled over to the side of this highway, turned on the seat, grabbed him and gave him a big kiss—out of pure gratitude for being kind to her granny, of course—what would he do? How would he react?

How would *she* react? Because just thinking about it was giving her sweaty palms.

"How did it go with the family?" Laura asked.

Katy switched the telephone to the other ear and held it in place with her shoulder. "Fine."

"Fine? Just fine? Didn't they believe the two of you were a couple?"

"They believed it, all right. They were ready to pick a date."

"Then it worked!"

"It worked too well. A bunch of them are coming up for my birthday. That means I'll have to produce Dylan, because they all act like he hung the moon."

"Katy Andrews, you sound positively surly. Isn't this what you wanted to happen? Now your grandmother can die happy."

"My grandmother looks like she's going to outlive us all."

"Oh." A pause and then Laura giggled. "Does that mean you'll have to marry the man to keep from being exposed as a fake?"

"I'd rather *be* exposed," Katy shot back. "Can we change the subject, please? How's the little mother-to-be?"

"Big as a house and still growing," Laura said cheerfully. "So will you and Dylan be going to the big Harvest Day celebration Saturday?"

"Sheesh, I forgot all about that."

"Now that I've reminded you..."

"I don't know, Laura," Katy hedged. "Maybe."

"Everyone will be there. It'll look funny if you don't."

"Thanks for pointing that out."

Laura laughed. "I even like you when you get cross," she said. "See you Saturday at Harvest Day."

Katy finished up the story she'd been working on when Laura called, but found herself thinking about the community-wide event between sentences. When she'd finished the story, she hesitated with her hand on the telephone.

What the heck. She picked up the handset and dialed.

Fortunately, all she got was his answering machine. "Howdy, folks. This is Dylan, but I'm not really here. I'm out on the north forty punchin' them dogies.

You'll have to leave one of those dad-blamed messages at the beep.''

"Oh, for heaven's—Dylan, that's the corniest message I ever heard. Listen, you wouldn't want to go to Harvest Day Saturday, would you? Laura thinks we should, but what does she know? Naw, you've got better things to do with your time. Forget I called.''

She hung up, satisfied with herself. Now she could tell Laura she'd done her best.

"You have reached the home of Katy Andrews. I may be out or I may be screening calls, but you can leave a message at the beep.''

"Hi, Katy, it's your beloved. I've decided to take you up on your gracious invitation to Harvest Day. I'll pick you up at ten. And by the way, your message, although far from corny, is the dullest thing I ever heard. Just wanted to share that with you.''

He started to hang up, changed his mind and added, "This is Dylan, in case you can't tell your beloveds apart.''

Then he *did* hang up, and he was laughing.

"I don't want to do the cake walk! What would I do with a cake even if I won?'' Wandering around and hoping to end up on the winning circle when the music stopped wasn't her idea of a good time.

"Did it ever occur to you that you could give it to me?''

Katy and Dylan stood nose-to-nose in front of the ticket table before said cake walk, "discussing'' at the tops of their lungs. She saw the ticket lady smiling and tried to tame her tone.

"I didn't think you liked cake," she said through gritted teeth.

"I don't much. I want one of us to win a pie."

"Then we should be standing in front of the *pie* walk," she said reasonably.

"Hey, do I make the rules? Right over there in the middle of all those cakes are a couple of pies and I want one."

"Then *you* win one!"

"If we both play, I'll win twice as fast." He tossed two blue tickets in front of the ticket lady, grabbed Katy's hand and pulled her up the steps of the bandstand while cake walkers applauded a small boy holding an enormous chocolate cake.

"Take your places for the cake walk, everybody!"

"Pie walk!" Dylan hollered. He hung onto Katy's hand as if he thought she might escape. "Are you with me, babe?"

"Sure she is!" a tall, skinny kid yelled. He pushed his baseball cap back on a head of wild red hair. "Not!"

"See there?" Dylan hissed at her. "Nobody's gonna believe we're a couple if you don't start treating me a little better. And your family's gonna show up next weekend and then where will you be?"

"Oh, all right." She shook off his hand and stepped onto one of the tape circles on the floor. "See, I'm cooperating."

"Hooray!" The skinny kid applauded. "Katy's cooperating!"

The music began and the cake walkers stepped off with much giggling and maneuvering. Katy strolled along, not in the least interested in winning a pie or a cake, but enjoying herself just the same. She'd finally admitted, if only to herself, that she actually *enjoyed* baiting Dylan and parrying his retorts. The guy was really quite quick with the comebacks. What had he said...? He liked a fair fight.

Well, so did she. But if she was wise she wouldn't start liking it too much because—

The music stopped and in a mad rush, everyone seemed to converge on Katy. Jostled and bumped, she planted her feet firmly and tried to stare down the horde.

"Hey, watch who you're pushing!" She planted hands on hips and gave the offenders an icy glare.

"Katy!" Dylan picked her up and hugged her. "You won!"

"I did?" Blinking, she looked down and found her feet firmly planted in the winner's circle. "Good grief, I *did* win."

"Yes indeedy, you won this beautiful angel-food cake." One of the game workers hurried forward holding the cake outstretched.

A universal groan went up, and Dylan said, "But I wanted to win the pie—I mean, I wanted my *girl* to win the pie."

"I'm not a girl, Dylan Cole, I'm a *woman!*"

"And a lot of woman you are, too." He patted her arm but kept his gaze on the confused cake lady. "Please, Mrs. Brown, could we trade that in for a pie instead?"

"Well, I—I don't know—" She looked around for guidance.

"Give 'em the pie!" someone yelled. "They've earned it in entertainment value alone."

The crowd burst out laughing and Katy laughed along, somewhat gingerly.

"In that case—" Mrs. Brown traded in the cake on a tall lemon meringue and presented it to Katy. "Congratulations!" she said. "Now can we *please* get on with our game?"

"Absolutely." Katy, holding the pie, turned to leave.

"Aren't you forgetting something?" Dylan asked plaintively.

"I don't think so," she said innocently.

"The pie?"

"What about it?"

"Aren't you going to give it to me?"

An expectant hush settled over the cake walkers, as if they were all holding their breath. Katy balanced the pie on one hand, thinking that she wouldn't dare...she truly wouldn't dare....

The tall skinny kid broke the tension-packed silence. "Why don't you give it to *her* instead?" he called out, his tone suggestive.

Dylan wore an amused expression that told her that he was enjoying this as much as she was. But he didn't have the pie. She did.

He started forward. She took a step back, suddenly uncertain.

"Don't come a step closer or the pie gets it!" she warned him.

"You wouldn't destroy an innocent pie." He took another step.

Again she retreated. "I mean it, Dylan. This is my pie and the only way you can have it is—"

"We'll see about that!"

He moved so fast she had no time to react, snatching the pie out of her hand and holding it aloft. At the same time he wrapped his other arm around her waist and dragged her close.

"Don't struggle," he warned. "You're within bursting radius of this pie."

"Don't threaten me! I'll call the pie police!"

"While you're at it," he said, "call the kissing police, because I'm just about to put down a deposit on this pie."

And before she knew what was happening, he was kissing her.

CHAPTER FIVE

KATY WAS SIMPLY having too much fun to offer even token resistance. To the accompaniment of cat calls and applause, she wrapped her arms around Dylan's neck and kissed him back.

Which was an awful mistake, she quickly realized, for then he immediately bent her backward over his arm and accelerated the kiss with enthusiasm. This was more than she'd bargained for. By the time he lifted his head, she was practically gasping.

He lowered the pie he'd been holding in the air. "Safe and sound," he announced. "I am a man of many talents."

"Boy, I'll say!" The words just burst from her lips before she could stop them.

Over spontaneous applause, the loudspeaker boomed: "Take your places, folks!" Recorded music began to play. "Here we go, step right up for the cake walk...."

Taking Katy's hand, Dylan led her down the steps to ground level. Once there, he gave her a crooked smile.

"Thanks," he said.

She blinked. "For kissing you?"

"Yep—for kissing me with Brandee and that gang of women looking on. I don't know how you knew she was there, but I appreciate your cooperation."

So that's all it had been: an opportunity to discourage women. "Any time," she said, holding back when he would have led her away. "Where are you dragging me?"

"I saw Matt and Laura and the kids heading in this direction. I thought they might like to share my pie."

"*Your* pie?"

"What's yours is mine."

"And vice versa!"

They were still arguing the issue of pie ownership when they tracked down the Reynolds family, waiting in line at the carousel.

Laura and Katy sat at a picnic table and watched Jessica and Zach enjoy the rise and fall of the carousel with squeals of approval. The two men stood nearby, holding the pie between them while they ate directly from the tin with plastic spoons.

Laura brushed at eyes damp from the after-effects of prolonged laughter. "I'd have paid to see you and Dylan hassling over that pie," she declared. "You two are the limit! You could fight over how high is up."

"I think we've already done that."

Laura's expression turned mischievous. "So, is he a good kisser?"

"Laura!"

"I suppose I shouldn't ask, but you know how pregnant women are—we just can't help ourselves."

Katy shook her head ruefully. "You are definitely pregnant. And you are my best friend...."

"Yes? Yes? Go on!"

"It was...all right."

"Just all right?" Laura looked disappointed.

"Okay, a little better than all right, actually."

"Now we're getting somewhere. How *much* better than all right?"

Katy groaned. "A lot better—a *whole* lot better. Laura, I must be losing my mind. Anyone but Dylan Cole!" And she put her head down on folded arms and wailed.

Dylan heard Katy's howl and looked up from the pie pan. "There she goes again," he said. "Everything is high drama with that woman."

Matt licked meringue off his spoon. "Never a dull moment, huh?"

Dylan hadn't thought of it in quite that way, but it sure was the truth. He nodded. "She's a helluva good sport, though. She'll try anything once."

"Twice if she likes it." Matt chuckled.

"Yeah." Dylan, remembering the kiss, was heartened. "As long as I've known her, you wouldn't think she could still surprise me...but she can."

Dylan looked at his friend with assessing eyes. "Sounds to me like the play-acting has taken a turn for the serious."

"What?" Dylan frowned.

"This phony courtship, designed to lead up to a phony engagement. I'm not so sure it's so phony any more."

"The hell it's not!" Dylan didn't realize he'd roared his denial until the women looked pointedly in his direction. He lowered his voice. "Listen, if you think I'm falling for little Katy Andrews, you've got another think coming. As my sainted grandmother would say, 'She'd drive a wooden man crazy.'''

And I'm not made of wood. He stifled a groan. If he was, he wouldn't be standing here eating pie but thinking about a certain green-eyed brunette who was ready for the kissing Olympics.

And glaring into the eyes of a friend who could barely summon the good grace not to laugh.

"I don't want to go to the movies," Katy said firmly. "There's nothing playing that is even faintly appealing to me."

"Well, la-dee-da," Dylan said. "Maybe there's something *I* want to see."

"I will *not* sit though one of those monster-destroys-the-world flicks. They are *too* ridiculous."

"Who died and made you a film critic?"

At the next table at the I Scream You Scream Ice Cream Shoppe, called the ISYS by locals, Roger Reedy nudged his wife Meredith in the ribs and chortled. "Listen to the love birds," he said, loud enough that the "love birds" couldn't miss hearing him. "Do you suppose there's trouble in paradise?"

Katy gave him a baleful glance; Meredith took that opportunity to wave. "You know what's wrong with you two?" she called.

Katy rolled her eyes. "I expect you're going to tell me."

"Naturally. The trouble with you two is, you've known each other too long. You should be more like Roger and me—spontaneous."

"That's right." Roger leaned forward earnestly. "We'd known each other about a month when we got married."

"Excuse me for saying so," Katy said with just a trace of sarcasm, "but did it ever occur to you that you just got lucky?"

Roger grinned broadly. "Of *course* we got *lucky*, but we made our own luck." He picked up his wife's hand. "I took one look at this woman and knew she was the one for me. If I'd waited until I got to know her better, know all the little irritating things—"

"What irritating things?" Meredith gave him her eagle-eyed attorney look.

"Nothing important, lover. I'm speaking in general terms."

"No, if I'm annoying you in some way I'd appreciate hearing about it."

Dylan gave Katy a significant glance. "Now look what you've started."

"I haven't started anything."

Roger's voice sounded slightly less lyrical. "If you insist, Meredith." He was beginning to look a trifle grim. "Do you realize that you only eat one thing at a time? If it's breakfast, you eat all the bacon. Then you eat all the eggs. Then you eat the toast. I find myself holding my breath, waiting for you to decide where you'll start. Sometimes I make little bets with myself."

"Oh, do you really?" Meredith must look this way in the courtroom: completely focused. "I would think that would be a point for my side, considering how you mash everything together and put catsup on top.

Why should I go to the trouble of cooking gourmet meals when all you're going to do is—''

"Meredith, sweetie, you're missing the point. Until you forced me to confess, your eating habits were an irritant I carefully kept hidden.''

"Irritant! Irritant?'' Meredith rose from the small round table, planting her hands on its surface and leaning forward aggressively. "Okay, lover boy, if you want to match irritants—''

Katy jabbed Dylan with an elbow. "If I want to see a fight, I don't have to come here to do it. Are you ready to go?''

"Go where?''

"Away from here!''

He followed her out of the ice cream parlor, popping the last bite of his cone into his mouth. "Actually,'' he said, "Roger's got a good point. Familiarity does breed contempt.''

"Is that your polite way of saying that you have nothing but contempt for me? Because I think contempt at first sight is just as likely. If I could remember when I first saw you, I'm sure that would support such a position.''

"All I'm saying is that it's easier to love someone you don't know, because when you get to know them, they'll disappoint you anyway.'' He led her toward his pickup parked at the curb.

"And all I'm saying is that it's better to discover feet of clay before the ceremony, not wait until after.''

They climbed into the cab of the truck, still arguing. Instead of starting the vehicle, he rested his hands on the wheel and looked at her over his shoulder.

"So what are you waiting for?" she asked.

"You to tell me where we're going," he said. "Apparently it's *not* to the movies."

"Not when the only things playing are monsters, outer space and kid flicks."

"I could take you home."

"Don't sound so hopeful." She glared at him. "Let me think.... We could go get a drink at the Painted Pony."

"You want a drink?"

"No."

"Three strikes and you're out."

"We could go...go bowling."

"Do you like to bowl?"

"Not really."

"Me, either. Strike two."

She sighed in exasperation. "Why do I always have to come up with all the ideas? You could help, you know."

"Okay, how about—"

"I've got it!" She snapped her fingers. "Let's go see if Laura and Matt are home. Actually, that's not a bad idea. I'd like to hear their take on long court-ships versus short ones."

"Why? In our case, that's like asking what they think about margarine versus imitation butter. They're both phony as hell so what difference does it make?"

"Purely a philosophical inquiry on my part," she said airily. "Besides, I haven't seen Laura since Harvest Day. With the baby due in just a couple of weeks, I want to know how she's doing."

"Good idea," Dylan agreed. He started the pickup

and hung a U-turn right in the middle of town. ''Boy, I sure wouldn't want to be in Matt's shoes on this one.''

''I thought you liked kids,'' Katy purposely misunderstood.

''I do, but I don't want any part of bringing them into the world.''

''I see. You're willing to be around at the beginning but don't ask you to participate in the ending.''

''That's not fair, Katy. Birthing babies is woman's work.''

She gave a disgusted grunt and slumped down in her seat. ''Or as I told Laura, you couldn't melt Dylan and pour him into a delivery room. I sure do pity any woman who'd marry a man like that.''

''Oh, yeah? For your information, I got women lined up.''

''Oh, yeah? Then why did you ask me to help you discourage all of them?''

''Because I knew you were in a bind yourself, and because I didn't have to worry about you getting any ideas.''

''Ideas about what?''

He pulled into the Reynolds' driveway and braked. ''Ideas about me. Ideas about making a phony arrangement the real thing.''

''I'd cut my wrists first!''

''And I'd cut my throat!''

They glared at each other.

Then Katy drew a deep breath. ''Have we got that out of our systems? No need to subject Laura to your childish outbursts.''

"My—!" He counted to ten very quickly, then pasted on a false smile. "Okay, I'll concede the point about Laura. She's probably in there resting with her loved ones around her. Why ruin her evening?"

"We should have brought a quart of ice cream."

"Now you think of it."

"Why do I have to think of everything?"

They argued right up to the back door, where each took a deep breath and pasted on smiles before knocking.

Laura was not "resting with her loved ones around her." She opened the door with a sheen of sweat on her face, one of her husband's old T-shirts covering most of her, a sponge in her hand.

Katy stared. "What in the world are you doing?"

"Mopping the floor." Laura stepped aside for them to enter. "I'm glad you're here. Dylan, could you shove that refrigerator back into place for me?" She indicated the huge white appliance pulled out several feet from the wall. A bucket with a mop handle extending from it sat nearby.

"Sure." Dylan looked around and frowned. The room was a mess with cabinets open, cleaning supplies all over the place. "What the heck do you think you're doing, Laura?" he inquired. "Big as you are, I'm surprised you can walk, let alone scrub floors."

Katy punched him on the arm. "Dylan, you dolt! That's rude!"

He rubbed his arm, wondering what it was with women that made them so sensitive to the truth. "But she *is* big."

Laura laughed. "She sure is." She patted her belly. "Junior here just keeps growing and growing."

"Junior?" Dylan repeated. "It's a boy, then?"

"That was just a figure of speech." Laura gestured for them to sit down. "I told the doctor I didn't want to know because I don't care. Boy or girl, we'll love it just the same."

"Well, sure." Dylan knew that much. Instead of sitting, he crossed to push the refrigerator back into place.

"Can I get you two something to drink?" Laura asked.

Katy sprang to her feet. "Let me. You sit down and relax, Laura." She glanced around, frowning. "Where is everyone? Surely you're not here alone?"

Laura waved her friend away and moved toward the refrigerator, now back in its rightful place. "It's easier for me to move than it is to sit still." She opened the door and pulled out three cans of soda, carrying them to the table. "As for the kids—Matt took them to a movie."

"You're alone?" Katy looked horrified at the thought.

"Katy, dear, I'm alone every day when Matt goes to work and the kids go to school. Besides, they were driving me crazy."

"Crazy how?" Katy snapped the ring on her soda can.

"Very much like you'd do if I'd let you." Laura rolled her eyes. "I'm not sick, I'm not an invalid, I don't need to be waited on hand and foot. When people hover over me, it makes me nuts."

"I don't know." Katy darted an accusing glance at Dylan, "I think I might kind of like it now and then."

"Trust me, you wouldn't." Laura took a sip of soda. "Anyway, right after they left I got this overwhelming urge to—to *do* something. So I made peanut-butter fudge. Matt doesn't like chocolate, you know."

"Fudge! It's not even Christmas." Katy seemed shocked at such a breach in holiday etiquette.

"You don't have to wait for Christmas to make candy. Would either of you like a piece?"

Dylan avoided looking at Katy. "I kinda like fudge."

Laura swayed to her feet and headed for the counter. She seemed unable to remain still for more than a minute or two. "Anyway, after I made the fudge I was still kind of bored so I decided to clean the kitchen. Guess I got carried away." She picked up a plate. "To what do I owe the pleasure of your company?"

Katy gave Dylan a warning glance. "We were just over at the ISYS and witnessed a rather appalling display of marital manners," she explained primly.

Laura set the plate of candy in the middle of the table. "By whom?"

"Roger and Meredith Reedy."

"You're kidding. I thought they were still deliriously happy."

Laura lowered herself back into her chair. Dylan noticed that despite the pleasant coolness of the evening, the sheen of perspiration still covered her face.

Without commenting on that, he reached for a piece of the beige fudge.

"Yeah," he said, "they *were* happy until they ran into Hurricane Katy. When we left, they were going at it pretty hot and heavy."

"Dylan, you promised we wouldn't get Laura worked up about that stupid incident."

"Don't worry, Katy." Laura patted her friend's hand. "I can use a good diversion right about now."

Dylan thought her breathing sounded a bit heavy, but it wasn't any of his business. "Katy's always good for a diversion," he agreed. "Anyway, turns out Mr. and Mrs. Reedy bug the hell out of each other on a regular basis, but neither intended to mention it until our girl here got them going."

"That's not what we came to discuss," Katy said, her green eyes snapping. "What we want to know is, do you think marriages have a better chance of working when people have known each other for a long time or when it's love at first sight?"

Laura licked her lips and Dylan noticed she was breathing lightly, almost in pants.

"Let me give that the attention it deserves," she said. "First of all, I *do* believe in love at first sight."

"Aha!" Dylan shot a triumphant glance at Katy. "I told you it's better to get married before you know the other person's failings and now Laura is agreeing with me."

Laura laughed. "No, I'm not! Even with love at first sight, I think you should wait until you really get to know each other."

"Aha!" Now it was Katy's turn to look triumphant. "And then when you get to know each other's failings, you've still got time to avoid a fatal commitment."

Dylan pounded his soda can on the table. "What are you talking about, Katy, marriage or suicide?"

"Whatever you want to call it!"

"Children, children!" Laughing, Laura held up her hands for order. "You two are the most wonderful diversion in the world."

Katy looked sheepish. "We're not upsetting you, are we? We promised we wouldn't get into a fight and look at us."

"Of course, you're not upsetting me. But to get back to your question—I'd say it depends."

"On what?" Katy wanted to know.

"The couple. It's a case of whatever works."

"You don't want to take sides," Dylan guessed.

"That's right."

He saw the way she laid her hands tenderly over the upper swell of her abdomen, the way her lips trembled when she smiled. She sure was acting funny, but who could explain a pregnant woman?

As if to confirm his judgment, Laura rose yet again. "If you don't mind, I think I'd like to keep on with my cleaning. I just have this sense of urgency, like I really ought to get everything in tiptop shape."

"Would you like us to go?" Katy glanced at Dylan, who nodded.

"Please don't," Laura said quickly. "I'm actually glad you dropped by because..."

"Because what?" Katy urged. She picked up her can of soda.

"Because," Laura said softly, "I'm in labor. Until Matt and the kids get back——"

"You're in labor!" Katy shot to her feet, wild-eyed. "Why didn't you say so? My gosh, we've got to get you to the hospital. Can you walk to Dylan's pickup? Should we call the ambulance?"

"Calm down!" Laura looked amused. "There's no hurry. I've got plenty of time."

Dylan, who devoutly hoped that was true, was more than willing to take her word for it. Katy wasn't as easily convinced.

"How do you know? Laura, I really don't think you should wait for them."

"I know because I've been there and done that," Laura said firmly. "I had Zach all alone and I'm not going to do that again. I'm going to wait for Matt *no matter what.*" She looked fiercely determined when she said it, then added more calmly, "Now I have my best friend and my husband's best friend to keep me company while I wait. Am I a lucky woman or what?"

Dylan was beginning to feel a little queasy. He stumbled to his feet. "Maybe I should go find Matt for you and bring him back. You said he took the kids to the m-movie?"

"Dylan Cole, you sit back down in that chair." Katy pointed imperiously to the seat he'd just vacated. "Laura will tell us what she wants done." She frowned. "Won't you? Because if you think we should track them down——"

"I want you to stay right here and amuse me, just as you've been doing."

"We can do that." Katy glanced at Dylan. "Right, Mr. Macho?"

Dylan groaned. "Hell, yes! I'm no quitter."

"That's great," Laura said warmly. "While we're waiting, I really want to keep busy. Dylan, if you'd put all that stuff back in the cleaning closet...and Katy, maybe you'd like to wash out the pans and utensils I used to make the candy? And I'll just—"

Huffing and puffing, she reached for the mop handle, her movements ponderous but determined.

Katy and Dylan looked at each other and her expression made him wonder which of them was the most panicked. They were out of their depth but what the heck; Laura knew what she was doing, right?

Right?

"There!" Laura surveyed her sparkling kitchen with approval. "At least I know I won't be leaving my family with a mess."

"It's beautiful," Katy said.

Dylan nodded agreement. He seemed to have gotten over his initial shock. Katy wondered how he'd react if Laura's labor suddenly intensified and they ended up having to, God forbid, deliver the baby.

In fact, she wondered how *she* would react. In theory, she knew the basics; if put to the test, she had no idea how she'd perform. Even as she watched, Laura gasped and her belly seemed to move beneath Matt's old gray T-shirt.

"Laura, honey," Katy said anxiously, "don't you think it's time we either went looking for Matt or got you to the hospital? It seems to me those contractions are coming closer and closer.''

The contraction passed and Laura straightened with a strained smile. ''That's what they're supposed to do. Don't worry I—'' She turned her back and walked away but Katy knew what was happening.

''We've got to get this stubborn woman to the hospital,'' she said under her breath. She added more loudly, ''Laura, do you have a bag packed or something?''

''Yes.'' Laura's voice sounded muffled. ''It's in the front closet, but I'm not going until Matt gets here.''

''Okay, how about this. We'll call your doctor and tell him you'll be coming in soon, and then Dylan will go in search of the missing—''

''Mama! Mama, the movie was great!''

The front door burst open and Jessica bounded inside, Zach on her heels. ''It was the best Disney movie ever!'' she exclaimed.

''Uh-uh.'' Zach stopped short. ''My favorite was that Aladdin one. But this one was good, too.''

Matt appeared behind the children, shooing them further into the room. He carried a pink-and-white checked paper bag with the ISYS logo. When he looked at his wife, his smile slipped.

''Laura, are you all right? You look—''

''Fine,'' she said quickly. ''I feel fine, too.'' She licked her lips. ''Uhh…Katy and Dylan were just about to pull out my suitcase for the trip to the hospital.''

All the color seemed to leave Matt's face. Without another word, he tossed the bag of ice cream to

Dylan, walked straight to his wife and took her in his arms as if he could absorb the tremors that shook her. For a long moment, he buried his face in the blond hair tumbling around her shoulders.

When he straightened, he seemed completely in control again.

Both kids stood there staring at their parents with wide eyes. Jessica said in a voice filled with awe, "Is it time?"

"Almost." Laura's smile seemed completely unforced. "You know what to do, right?"

"Right!" Jessica turned to Zach. "You remember. We're to call Mrs. Brown and ask her to come over right away."

"That's correct. Then what do you do?"

"Anything she tells us!" The kids shouted it in unison. Jessica added, "But Daddy will call us from the hospital as soon as he knows if we have a baby sister or a baby brother."

Matt slid an arm around Laura's waist, half supporting her. "That's right, because when we know that, we have to discuss a name."

Zach hopped up and down in delight. "It's gonna be a boy," he predicted. "I vote for Barney."

Jessica groaned. "You can't name our baby brother after a purple dinosaur! Get real! Besides, it'll be a girl and we'll name her—"

"Sorry, kids," Matt cut them off. "I think your mother and I had better be moving. Katy, will you stay here with the kids until Mrs. Brown arrives?"

"Of course. Don't give it a thought."

"I'm really grateful to the two of you for standing

in for me,'' Matt went on. "It's still a week or two early—''

"Is that a problem?'' Dylan cut in.

"No, no,'' Laura assured him. "Due dates are nothing more than educated guesses anyway. We—'' She sucked in her breath and looked at her husband. "I...think we probably should...get going.''

"I'll grab the suitcase.'' Dylan darted toward the hall closet.

"I'll get the big sister and big brother bathed and ready for bed.'' Katy turned to the children. "Kiss your mom and pop good-bye. Next time you see them you'll be a family of five instead of a family of four.''

That twinge of envy she felt came from being a family of one.

CHAPTER SIX

"So I DON'T THINK we should have to go to bed until Daddy calls and tells us the baby's born," Jessica concluded a lengthy argument. She looked expectantly at Katy.

Who yawned. "Jessica Reynolds, it's past ten o'clock now. Consider yourself lucky I let you stay up this long." She frowned. "I wonder what's keeping Mrs. Brown?"

"She'll be along soon," Dylan predicted. That Jessica was a real talker! The girl had been carrying on a non-stop monologue for the last ten minutes. Zach was the smart one; he'd tuned his sister out and lay dozing on the sofa, while Katy feigned interest.

Or maybe she really was interested. Both talker and talkee were female, after all.

Yawns, however, were catching. Dylan let loose with one of his own. Katy saw it and snapped to attention.

"If you're bored, you don't have to wait," she said. "I'll watch the kids until the sitter arrives."

"What makes you think I'm—"

"You yawned."

"So what? You yawned first. Are *you* bored?"

"Certainly not." She sniffed imperiously. "But women are just naturally more interested in this sort of thing—you know, babies being born. Far be it from me to—''

The pealing of the doorbell cut her off mid-tirade and he went to answer. Mrs. Brown stood there, all smiles beneath the porch light. Dylan let her in, then followed her back to the family room.

''Oh, my goodness!'' the grandmotherly woman exclaimed. ''Is it time already?''

Jessica looked suspicious. ''Time for babies to be born or time for kids to go to bed?''

Mrs. Brown laughed. ''Both, I would say. Wake up your little brother and—''

''I'll carry him,'' Dylan interrupted quickly.

Mrs. Brown shook her head. ''No need. He's used to walking.''

''I *want* to carry him.'' Dylan stepped up to the sofa, leaned down and eased the sleeping boy into his arms. Straightening, he looked at the fair hair and the soft little face. Something stirred inside him and for a moment, he didn't understand.

Then when he did, he didn't like it. Because although he might hunger for a son and heir, he *didn't* hunger for a wife.

''Dylan,'' Katy said softly, ''Mrs. Brown is waiting.''

''Oh, yeah, sure.'' Carrying the sleeping boy, Dylan followed the babysitter down the hallway, wondering at the black magic that had made him, just for a moment, think of Katy Andrews with a desire that clenched his gut.

Anyone but her, he thought, lowering the boy into

Play **LUCKY HEARTS** for this.

exciting FREE gift!
**This surprise mystery gift
could be yours free**

when you play **LUCKY HEARTS!**
...then continue your lucky streak
with a sweetheart of a deal!

1. Play Lucky Hearts as instructed on the opposite page.
2. Send back this card and you'll receive brand-new Harlequin Romance® novels. These books have a cover price of $3.50 each in the U.S. and $3.99 each in Canada, but they are yours to keep absolutely free.
3. There's no catch! You're under no obligation to buy anything. We charge nothing—ZERO—for your first shipment. And you don't have to make any minimum number of purchases—not even one!
4. The fact is thousands of readers enjoy receiving books by mail from the Harlequin Reader Service®. They enjoy the convenience of home delivery...they like getting the best new novels at discount prices, BEFORE they're available in stores...and they love their *Heart to Heart* subscriber newsletter featuring author news, horoscopes, recipes, book reviews and much more!
5. We hope that after receiving your free books you'll want to remain a subscriber. But the choice is yours—to continue or cancel, any time at all! So why not take us up on our invitation, with no risk of any kind. You'll be glad you did!

- ♦ **Exciting Harlequin romance novels—FREE!**
- ♦ **Plus an exciting mystery gift—FREE!**

YES!

I have scratched off the silver card. Please send me the 2 FREE books and gift for which I qualify. I understand I am under no obligation to purchase any books, as explained on the back and on the opposite page.

With a coin, scratch off the silver card and check below to see what we have for you.

HARLEQUIN'S

LUCKY HEARTS GAME

316 HDL CY3Q

116 HDL CY3F
(H-R-03/00)

NAME (PLEASE PRINT CLEARLY)

ADDRESS

APT.#   CITY

STATE/PROV.   ZIP/POSTAL CODE

Twenty-one gets you 2 free books, and a free mystery gift!

Twenty gets you 2 free books!

Nineteen gets you 1 free book!

Try Again!

Offer limited to one per household and not valid to current Harlequin Romance® subscribers. All orders subject to approval.

DETACH AND MAIL CARD TODAY!

The Harlequin Reader Service®—Here's how it works:

Accepting your 2 free books and gift places you under no obligation to buy anything. You may keep the books and gift and return the shipping statement marked "cancel." If you do not cancel, about a month later we'll send you 6 additional novels and bill you just $2.90 each in the U.S., or $3.34 each in Canada, plus 25¢ delivery per book and applicable taxes if any.* That's the complete price and — compared to cover prices of $3.50 each in the U.S. and $3.99 each in Canada — it's quite a bargain! You may cancel at any time, but if you choose to continue, every month we'll send you 6 more books, which you may either purchase at the discount price or return to us and cancel your subscription.

*Terms and prices subject to change without notice. Sales tax applicable in N.Y. Canadian residents will be charged applicable provincial taxes and GST.

BUSINESS REPLY MAIL
FIRST-CLASS MAIL   PERMIT NO. 717   BUFFALO, NY

POSTAGE WILL BE PAID BY ADDRESSEE

HARLEQUIN READER SERVICE
3010 WALDEN AVE
PO BOX 1867
BUFFALO NY 14240-9952

NO POSTAGE
NECESSARY
IF MAILED
IN THE
UNITED STATES

the bed already turned back by the sitter. Anyone at all.

Except maybe Brandee Haycox.

Or his ex-wife—ah, to heck with it. He'd had a strange evening, that was all.

In the clear light of day, he'd see Katy for what she really was.

Whatever *that* might be.

"Just drop me off at the hospital," Katy instructed as they passed through the dark and sleeping streets of Rawhide. "I'll bum a ride home later, or Matt can take me once the baby comes."

"The hell I will."

She looked at him, surprised by his vehemence. In the glow of the instrument panel, he appeared downright foreboding. "Let me out here, then, if that will please you! I *don't* want to go home."

"Does it *look* as if I'm taking you home?"

She peered out the window at streets she'd known her entire life. "No," she admitted, "it looks like you're taking me to the hospital. But you just said, and I quote, 'the hell I will,' so I naturally assumed that meant you wouldn't."

"I meant I wouldn't drop you off at the hospital because I'm staying, too."

"Dylan, you know you don't have to do that."

"I *do* know, and I'd appreciate it if you stopped talking to me as if I were Jessica's age. I feel a little proprietary about that baby, I suppose you might say. I don't intend to go home until I know everything's turned out all right."

For a moment she stared at his strong profile, feeling herself weaken, soften.... She sighed. "I'm sorry. I just assumed—"

"You do a lot of that." He wheeled the pickup into the visitor parking lot up front. Switching off the lights, he turned toward her in the dark intimacy of the cab. "The way I see it, we kind of have a stake in this baby. I mean, we always did—Laura and Matt are the best. But after being there, seeing the grace with which Laura's handling this..."

"It was wonderful, wasn't it?" No more one-upsmanship for Katy. "I really admired the way she kept her wits about her. If my time ever comes—*when* my time comes—I hope I show half her class."

"You probably will," he said, so offhanded about it that it didn't even sound like a compliment. "One thing you've always had plenty of is guts." He turned toward the door. "Shall we go on inside and see if Matt's holding up half as well?"

Matt *wasn't* holding up quite as well as his wife. When he came out of the labor room to catch his breath, he looked ready to keel over.

Katy and Dylan, alone in the small waiting room, rushed to the expectant father's side.

"You okay?" Dylan pounded his friend on the back. "You look about ready to pass out."

Matt sucked in deep breaths, as if he'd never get enough oxygen into his lungs ever again. "Man," he muttered when he could talk again, "now I know why they call it *labor*. I'm standing around useless, and I'm exhausted just watching. How Laura can handle it like she does is a mystery to me." He pulled himself together. "I guess Mrs. Brown finally made it."

"Yes." Katy squeezed his hand.

"I appreciate you both being here, but you don't have to stay."

"We've already fought that one out," Dylan said. "Katy and I... we kind of feel we've got a special interest in this kid. We want to be sure he or she has arrived safely before we call it a night."

"Okay." Matt smiled for the first time. "The doctor's with Laura now. I'll let you know when they get ready to move her into the delivery room."

"Fine," Katy said. "In the meantime, we're here if you need us. Other than that, don't give us a single thought."

"You got it." He kissed the top of her head and wheeled around. "Cross your fingers!"

"*You* got it." Dylan crossed his fingers with a flourish. When he looked at Katy, it was with an affection that felt brand new. "Guess we might as well settle down to wait."

"Looks like." She led the way back inside the waiting room, looked around at the uninspired selection of vinyl chairs and small vinyl couch, then chose the couch. She yawned. "No, I'm not bored," she said quickly. "I'm sleepy."

Dylan glanced at the big clock over the door. "It's almost midnight. How long do babies take to be born?"

"Just as long as they want." Katy sank down on her spine in the corner of the couch. "I guess Matt will wake me when there's any news."

"Make that *us*—wake us when there's any news."

"Okay, sure." Drowsiness muffled her voice. "Just for the record, Dylan…"

"Yeah?" He peered at her suspiciously.

"You were a rock back there with Laura." Turning onto her side, she snuggled her legs beneath her, arm across the back of the sofa to cradle her head. Her eyelids drifted closed. "I was proud of you.…"

He sat for a long time, watching her sleep and wondering why her faint words of even fainter praise thrilled him so.

Then he moved to the opposite end of her small couch and settled down to grab a few winks himself.

"Hey, wake up! It's all over but the shoutin'!"

Katy opened one eye. All she saw was a blur of blue plaid. "Ummm?" she murmured.

"It's me, Matt. Wake up! The baby's here, in case you two are still interested."

Katy licked her lips and tried to pull her thoughts together. She'd fallen asleep on the hard vinyl of the small sofa in the waiting room. Why was she waking up with her cheek cradled against…

My God! She bolted upright. She'd been sleeping in Dylan's arms, her cheek against his heart…all warm and safe and… She stared at him, horrified.

His eyes finally opened, and he frowned and said, "Huh?"

Matt laughed, and his image finally came into focus for Katy.

"The baby's here," he said. "Mother and child are doing fine."

Dylan rubbed at his eyes. "Boy or girl?"

Matt's grin grew even wider. "Girl."

"Wow!" Dylan returned the smile. "That's great. Congratulations, buddy."

"Thanks." Matt looked exhausted, but his happiness still managed to lift him above that minor annoyance.

"What time is it?" Katy asked, peering through foggy eyes at the big clock on the wall. "Five-thirty a.m.? Holy cow, I'd better get home, Dylan."

"Yeah, of course." He sat up, shoving his hair away from his face with both hands.

"Would you guys like to see mother and baby first?"

At Matt's soft invitation, Dylan and Katy both bolted to their feet with a resounding *yes!* A little awed, they followed the new father down the hall the few short steps to the nursery window. Baby Reynolds, the only infant in the three-bed nursery, lay in a clear plastic bassinet which unaccountably made Katy think of Cinderella's glass slipper. A pink blanket swaddled the sleeping baby, and a gauze cap covered any hair she might have. Her tiny rosebud mouth moved hungrily.

Katy glanced at Dylan; he was frowning.

"Why's she so red and wrinkly?" he asked. "Is something wrong with her?"

"Heck, no!" Matt recoiled as if his newest daughter had just been insulted. "That's how all babies look when they're first born. Tell him, Katy."

"Absolutely," Katy said, although she had limited experience with new babies. "She'll outgrow it."

"I hope," Dylan muttered beneath his breath.

Matt glowered at his friend, then led them on to an open door through which they found Laura, obviously exhausted but with a queen-sized smile on her face.

"I can't believe you two waited all night," she greeted Katy and Dylan. "You're the best friends! Did you see her? Isn't she beautiful?"

"She's gorgeous." Katy leaned down to give her friend a hug and a kiss on the cheek. "Her mother's pretty great, too."

Laura laughed. "It was nothing. I'm a little tired, that's all, but much too excited to sleep." Her gaze met that of her husband. "Did you tell them, honey?"

"Tell us what?" Katy looked from one to the other.

Matt shook his head. "I thought you'd want to do it."

"Do what?" Dylan demanded. "You're making me nervous, here."

"Don't be," Laura said quickly. "We're just talking about our baby's name."

"What is it?" Katy asked. "Did you follow Jessica's advice?"

"Nope." Matt looked so happy and at peace, now that it was all over. Sitting on the side of Laura's bed, he lifted her hand and pressed it to his lips before going on. "Circumstances kinda changed our plans."

"Stop teasing, honey." Laura patted his knee. She took a deep breath. "We've decided to name her Katy Cole Reynolds. Now isn't that a nice name?"

Katy lost her breath in astonishment. "You're naming her after *us*?"

"Can you think of anyone more deserving?" Matt cocked his head and waited for an answer.

Which Katy was beyond giving. She was so touched by the gesture that it rendered her speechless. Tears blurring her vision, she turned toward Dylan.

He looked completely stunned. "Gee," he murmured, "that's quite a responsibility, having a kid named after you."

"We thought you were up to it," Laura said, a smile tugging at the corners of her mouth. "Katy Cole will never forget who stood by her mama's side the night she was born."

"Katy Cole." Dylan repeated the two names.

At the sound of her name linked with his, Katy's stomach clenched. It had a nice ring to it, a *real* nice ring. Which caused a horrible possibility to leap out at her.

Could she possibly be falling for Dylan Cole?

Laura yawned and tried to cover it, but Matt saw and turned to his guests.

"I think it's time we all cleared out and let the new mama get her beauty rest," he suggested, "not that she needs it. She's the most gorgeous woman in the world already."

"Yes," Laura agreed, "and the moon really *is* made of green cheese." But she didn't bother to deny her obvious need for rest.

Dylan and Katy turned toward the door. "I'll drop by later," she promised.

"If you have time." Laura snuggled down into her

pillow. "We'll be going home tomorrow so you can always come by the house."

"Wow! I can't believe you only spend one day in the hospital."

"Modern medicine." Laura yawned again.

Matt still stood by her side, holding her hand. "I'm really wound up," he said. "You guys want to come over to the house and have breakfast? We can tell the kids and maybe I can calm down a little."

Dylan glanced at Katy. She looked different, somehow; softer, more acquiescent. Maybe babies did that to women. "Want to?" he asked.

"Sure, if Matt means it." She glanced at him. "We wouldn't want to be in the way."

"You won't be. Go on ahead." He turned back toward his wife. "I'll be right behind you."

"What'll we tell the kids, if they're up?"

"That the baby's been born and Daddy's comin' home to tell them all about it."

"We can do that," Dylan agreed.

He slipped an arm around Katy's shoulders and together they walked through a hospital stirring for another day: nurses hurrying past, breakfast carts taking up the middle of the hall, orderlies pushing gurneys. Moving as one, they walked out the front door and into the visitor parking lot. At the black pickup truck, they halted.

Dylan waited for her to step away from him, to break the contact as he was loathe to do.

She didn't. Instead, she turned toward him and pressed her face against the curve of his shoulder, her arms around his waist. After a stunned moment, he wrapped her in a snug embrace.

It took him another moment to realize she was crying.

"Hey, what's this?" He touched her chin, forcing her face up so he could look at her. "What's wrong?"

She tried to draw her chin away, to hide her face again, but he wouldn't let her.

"Don't look at me," she said in a strangled voice. "I don't cry pretty."

He'd never heard anything so silly in his life. Why would a person care if they "cried pretty"? "You cry great," he said. "Wanna tell me why?"

"B-because...I'm so touched. They named their baby after us. You and me, after years of annoying them with our petty squabbles—they named their baby Katy Cole."

"Has kind of a nice ring to it." He let her press her cheek against his chest again. Her head fit right under his chin in the nicest way. "I don't think I've ever seen two happier people."

"Me, either. Gosh, Dylan, the miracle of birth really *is*—a miracle, I mean."

She dug her fingers into his sides and he quivered, not from pain but from a sudden longing to possess this woman completely. As incredible as it seemed, Katy was turning him on in a major way.

Perhaps he, too, had been left vulnerable by that which they'd been honored to share. He'd have to think about it. Now he had to get them both over to the Reynolds house before one or the other of them said or did something that would come between them later.

She lifted her face to his. "You felt it, too—the magic. I'll bet you surprised yourself as much as you did me."

"You think guys don't have feelings?"

"That's not what I meant at all. I just—"

"We've got feelings, all right." Setting her aside, he fumbled in his jeans pocket and came out with the truck keys. "We just don't go around advertising them, is all."

"Well, you don't have to get all touchy." The old aggressive Katy surfaced quickly. "What am I supposed to do, Dylan, read your mind?" She climbed into the cab and scooted over quickly, as if she didn't want to risk touching him again. "Of course, with you that would be a short story."

"Ha-ha, Katy made a joke. I'll have you know, I'm as nuts about that baby as you are. She's got *my* name, too."

"Yes—second. She'll be called Katy, wait and see. Nobody calls a girl Cole."

"Oh, no? This one could be the first." Back on familiar footing, he steered toward the parking-lot exit. This was more like it.

They argued about the baby's name all the way to the Reynolds' house.

Mrs. Brown smiled but wouldn't be swayed into staying for breakfast. "I really must get home and feed my cats," she said, "but thanks for the invitation anyway. And congratulations again, Matt. A fine healthy girl! How much did she weigh?''

Katy wondered why she'd never thought to ask that most obvious of questions.

Matt smiled proudly. ''Seven pounds, ten ounces. And she's got lots of dark hair.''

''That'll all fall out,'' Mrs. Brown predicted.

Dylan looked appalled. ''Your baby's gonna be bald, Matt?''

Matt's face twisted with exasperation. ''Most babies lose the hair they're born with,'' he said in an annoyed tone. ''Jessica did, and look how good she turned out.''

''That's true,'' Dylan agreed. ''Still—''

''Dylan!'' Katy jabbed him with an elbow. ''I think Matt's getting a little sick of hearing you criticize his new daughter.''

''Criticize!'' Dylan looked horrified. ''I'm not *criticizing*. I just want to be sure everything's all right.''

''Everything's all right!'' Matt and Katy said it in unison—and with emphasis.

Chuckling, Mrs. Brown departed. By the time Jessica and Zach came stumbling into the kitchen, bacon sizzled in a skillet and the aroma of fresh coffee filled the air.

The two kids stopped short at sight of their father. Then they rushed forward simultaneously to throw themselves at him.

''Is the baby borned already?'' Zach demanded.

''We had a girl, right?'' Jessica added.

''Yes and yes.'' Matt hugged them both.

''When's Mama coming home?'' Zach demanded.

"Tomorrow. So is the baby."

"Oh, good!" Jessica clapped her hands in her excitement. "What's her name? Did you name her what I told you?"

At the stove turning bacon strips, Katy smiled at the girl's excitement. "What was that, Jess?"

"Summer Delight!"

Katy choked back her laughter. Dylan didn't; he guffawed.

Jessica glared. "What's wrong with that, Uncle Dylan? That's a very pretty name."

"Yes, it is," Matt agreed, "but it's not what we picked. I think you'll like our choice, honey, because it has a very special meaning. We named the new baby after Uncle Dylan and Aunt Katy, because they were here to help your mother when she needed it. Is that okay?"

"You named my sister Dylan Katy? I don't think so!" She glared at them all. "What will we call her? Girls aren't named Dylan!"

"She's got you there," Dylan inserted, choking on laughter.

Matt gave his friend a silencing glare before going on. "We named her Katy Cole Reynolds. How does that work for you?"

She considered. "Katy's not bad..." She glanced at the grown-up Katy and quickly added, "I mean, that's great. And Cole's better than Dylan, for a girl."

"You can just call her Katy," the grown-up Katy offered airily with an I-told-you-so glance at Dylan.

"Actually..." Matt grinned. "Laura and I are already calling her K.C. How does that work for you, Jess?''

She frowned, completely missing the point about initials. "Casey? I know a girl named Casey. She's real popular." She gave a sharp nod. "Casey's good, right Zach?"

Zach shrugged. "Sure, but can we *eat* now? All this talk makes me starved!"

"Gosh," Jessica said. "I can't believe you and Uncle Dylan stayed at the hospital *all night long.*"

Katy spooned scrambled eggs onto her plate. "It was kind of silly, since there was nothing more we could do. We just wanted to be there when the baby came."

"You, too, Uncle Dylan?"

He paused with a strip of bacon half-way to his mouth. "Sure. Why not?"

Jessica's expression became almost wily. "I guess you both like babies pretty much, then?"

"What's not to like?" Dylan popped the bacon into his mouth. "You overcooked this bacon, Katy."

"I certainly did not. I like it crisp."

"So do I, but I don't like it burned."

"If it's not up to your high standards—" She broke off, realizing they shouldn't squabble in front of the children. She added sweetly, "I mean, I'm so *terribly* sorry I've ruined your breakfast."

"You haven't." He reached for the platter of bacon again. "I've had worse."

Katy gritted her teeth but kept on smiling.

Jessica had watched the exchange with considerable interest. "You two sure fight a lot," she said.

"That's not fighting." Dylan finished what had to be his sixth slice of bacon.

Katy couldn't resist a dig. "If it's not fighting, what is it?"

Jessica leaned forward. "I know! Mama said it's lovers' quarrels." She frowned. "I don't really get it, though. Why would lovers fight all the time?"

"We're not lovers!" Katy darted a venomous glance at Dylan. "Far from it."

"How far?"

"Jessica," Matt said, "eat your breakfast and let Aunt Katy and Uncle Dylan eat theirs."

"But—"

"You ask too many questions, honey."

"But Daddy," she said sweetly, "isn't that how kids are supposed to learn? My teacher says, if you don't know something you should ask. She said there was no such thing as a dumb question—"

"—only dumb answers," Dylan inserted, rolling his eyes.

"You got that right," Katy shot at him. "Jessica, it's the difference between *personal* questions and— and other kinds."

"But if I have a question about you, Aunt Katy, shouldn't I ask *you?*"

"In theory, yes." She glanced uncomfortably at the two men but they obviously had no intention of offering her any help.

Jessica nodded. "That's what I thought. So when

are you and Uncle Dylan gonna get married and have a baby of your own?"

Dylan fought valiantly to keep from choking over his coffee. Katy sat as if in shock and Jessica waited for an answer to her question.

This, Dylan had to hear.

"Never!" Katy flung out the single word.

Her vehemence annoyed him. "So what's wrong with having my baby?" he demanded. "I bet it'd be a real cute little thing."

"Only if it took after its mother, who won't be me."

"Who, then?" Jessica asked.

Katy glared at Dylan. "Yes, who?"

"Somebody else, obviously," he said.

"But—" Jessica really looked confused now. "I thought you two would get engaged."

"What's engaged?" Zach inquired. To this point, he'd been eating steadfastly.

"That's before people get married, silly," Jessica said pompously.

"Why?" Zach scooped up the last of his scrambled eggs.

"So they can get presents and stuff. Don't you remember when Mama and Daddy got engaged, they had a party and people brought presents? Aunt Katy and Uncle Dylan don't want to miss that."

"We certainly do." Katy snatched Dylan's not-quite-empty plate away and stacked it on hers.

"Hey! I wasn't finished eating."

"You've had plenty."

"Then," Jessica pursued her point with unwavering dedication, "you're *not* gonna get engaged?"

Katy looked at Dylan and he saw her conflict; she didn't want to deny it and then, if that's what it took to pacify Brandee and Grandma, have to explain a change of heart to this inquisitive child.

So he finally came to her rescue. "We *might* get engaged," he said. "We've talked about it. But that's a long way from getting married and having a baby."

Jessica smiled as if she possessed some wonderful secret. "Not when people love each other," she said serenely. "Mama says then it's not very far at all."

CHAPTER SEVEN

MATT STOOD in the kitchen door, waving goodbye. Or maybe he more like *wavered* in the kitchen door. Dylan, who'd known the man forever, didn't think he'd ever seen such exhaustion in his face.

"Drop by late tomorrow if you want to see K.C. up close and personal," Matt called.

"You go to bed," Katy hollered back. "You look like death warmed over."

"That good, huh?" One final wave. "Thanks for cooking breakfast." He turned inside and shut the door.

Katy jumped into the pickup. "That's another fine mess you've gotten us into," she said once Dylan was seated beside her. "What did you mean, telling that sweet child that we might get engaged?"

"We might." He started the vehicle and pulled away from the curb.

"But it wouldn't be a true engagement."

"I know that and you know that. You want to explain it to Jessica, who's already got us married and raising a family?" Katy groaned. "She's the most *inquisitive* child."

"You got that right." He let out a weary sigh. "I don't know about you but I'm kinda wiped out myself. I didn't sleep all that great, wedged on that crummy plastic sofa."

"Funny." She gave him a slightly challenging glance. "I slept just fine."

"That's because you were sleeping on *me,* big old soft and cuddly me."

That drew a laugh. "I've got news for you, Dylan Cole. You're about as soft and cuddly as one of those longhorn steers you raise out at the Bear Claw."

"You wouldn't'a thought so, the way you were cuddled up and sawing logs last night."

"I hope you're not suggesting that I *snored*." She gave him a scathing glance.

"Only when you're sleeping."

"Dylan!" She banged a fist against his shoulder, saw he was laughing at her and subsided. "I don't know why I always let you get me like that," she grumbled.

"Neither do I, Katy. Neither do I." He pulled into her driveway and killed the engine. Sliding around on the seat, he faced her. "All kidding aside…"

Her expression turned suddenly serious. With a flash of intuition, he realized that she'd been keeping the more serious aspects of the night's events at bay.

"Last night," he said slowly, "was probably the greatest adventure of my life. I had no idea that the birth of a baby, especially when it's not even your own, could be so powerful."

"Powerful," she repeated softly. "Yes, that's what it was."

"Sharing it with *you* was powerful, too. I don't quite…understand what happened, but everything seems different today somehow."

She licked her lips, looking nervous. "I know what you mean."

"I think I'd better go away and figure it all out."

"Okay. I mean, me, too."

He smiled. "What's this? An agreeable Katy Andrews? Will wonders never cease?"

He reached out to cup her cheek with his open palm. Slowly and deliberately, so that she could withdraw at any moment if she chose, he leaned forward until his mouth nearly touched hers. He stared straight into those beautiful green eyes.

"Thanks for being there," he murmured.

"My pleasure," she murmured back...and the green eyes closed with a slow fluttering of long silky lashes.

He kissed her then, the way he'd been wanting to kiss her since they'd got into it so hot and heavy at the ice cream parlor—was that only last night? She yielded to him in a way he hadn't imagined she could. And then she was fully in his arms and one kiss became two and...

Someone was pounding on the window on the driver's side. Biting off a swear word, Dylan dragged his head around and yelled, "What!"

Amanda Willy stood there, sunlight gleaming off her carefully arranged white hair. At Dylan's response, she took a startled step back. Ashamed of himself, he rolled down the window. "I'm sorry, Mrs. Willy," he said. "What can I do for you?"

"Nothing," she shot back, "but Katy can." She spoke past him. "When you missed our nine o'clock appointment I was afraid something might be wrong so I came looking for you.''

"Oh, gosh," Katy groaned. "I forgot."

"Obviously, and I can see why." The old lady glared at Dylan. "If your grandmother could see you now, young man! What can you be thinking, bringing this girl home at ten in the morning?"

"I can explain," Katy said quickly.

"Let *him* explain!" Amanda was obviously on a tear. "In my day, a gentleman had more care for a woman's reputation."

"Mrs. Willy," Katy said desperately, "you don't understand. I didn't spend the night with Dylan—I mean I did, but—"

"Don't go on!" The old lady looked horrified.

"We spent the night at the hospital!" Katy sounded desperate to be believed. "Matt and Laura Reynolds had their baby last night, a little girl. Dylan and I—"

"Oh, I'm sorry! Shame on me for jumping to conclusions." Amanda looked horrified. "Dylan, dear boy, I should never have attacked you before the facts were in. But when I saw you grab this young woman…well, you understand."

He understood, all right. He understood that Amanda saw right through him, whether Katy did or not. She might be a senior citizen but she obviously recognized lust when she saw it.

Katy and Dylan, Jessica and Zach welcomed baby K.C. home the next day. Matt escorted Laura up the walk to the front door, the baby nestled in her arms.

The two kids could barely wait until their mother was ensconced on the family-room sofa to get a look at their new sister.

A smiling Laura laid the precious bundle on her thighs, the baby's feet toward her body. Carefully she peeled away the light blanket.

The children let out a mutual sigh of delight.

Laura nodded. "She *is* beautiful, isn't she!"

"No," Zach said, "but she's ours. Why's she so red and stuff, Mama?"

"Because she's so young." Laura picked up the little boy's hand and examined his fingernails. "Go wash those hands and you can touch her," she invited.

"Me, too?" Jessica held out her hands for inspection.

Laura nodded. "Sit right here beside me and I'll let you hold your baby sister."

Katy turned away from the maternal scene. "Matt!" she exclaimed in a disapproving whisper. "Is that a good idea? I mean, letting the kids handle her?"

"Laura knows what she's doing." He looked like a different man from the one they'd left here the previous day.

"I sure hope so." Katy could barely stand to watch. K.C. looked so fragile, so vulnerable. Katy's hands itched to touch that baby skin, caress the dark down on the little one's head. But she'd never been around such a tiny baby before and it scared her.

Not Jessica, though. "Look at me!" she crowed, holding K.C. carefully in the crook of her arm while her mother hovered beside her. "I think she likes me!"

K.C. was making faces, and little mewling noises, but Katy wasn't sure any of them indicated affection.

Zach rushed up, hands still damp. Laura took his little finger and guided it against the tiny palm. K.C.'s fingers convulsed and she hung on.

Zach's eyes filled with wonder. "She likes me," he said.

"Everybody likes you, sport." Matt patted the boy's shoulder.

Laura looked up with shining eyes. "Katy, would you like to hold your namesake?"

"Me?" Katy took two quick steps backward. "Uh...maybe later. I mean, of course I do, when she's older. Right now you're all having so much fun I wouldn't want to intrude."

Laura grinned at Dylan. "What that translates to is, 'I'm scared to death to touch that baby!'"

He grinned back. "I caught the translation."

"How about you? Do you want to hold her? Great big tough guy like you—show the little lady how it's done." Laura winked and took the baby from Jessica.

Dylan figured he must have turned a half-dozen shades paler in his panic. But Katy was watching him with jaundiced eye, and so were the kids, who hadn't been at all terrorized by a chunk of baby weighing less than a ten-pound sack of sugar.

He swallowed hard. "Okay, what do I do?"

Matt took K.C. from Laura. "Hold out your arms."

It took a lot of guts for Dylan to do as told. Matt placed K.C. in that cradle.

"Just remember," the daddy warned, "you've got to support her head. Other than that—hey, just think of her as some little dogie you picked up out on the range."

The comparison of this tiny bundle with a little lost calf tickled Dylan and made the transition a bit easier. "Then all I gotta do is swing her up over my saddle and carry her home to a nice warm stall and a bottle of milk," he said. The soft weight was like a feather in his embrace. K.C. was still making faces, her tiny mouth moving insistently and her eyes pressed into a tight line.

He knew what that meant. "I think she's hungry," he said, speaking low so as not to startle her.

"Don't worry," Laura advised. "When she wants to eat, she'll let us know in no uncertain terms."

He grinned. "Good lungs, huh." He glanced at Katy, who simply stood there staring as if she'd never seen a baby before. "Come on over and have a *good* look," he said, his tone bragging; after all, he was in charge here.

Katy edged closer. "She really is beautiful," she told the proud parents. Reaching out, she touched the wrinkled little hands with one gentle finger. K.C. turned blindly, mouth screwing up. Katy caressed the baby's cheek. "Her skin's so soft! I've never felt anything so soft."

Katy's green eyes glowed and her pink mouth trembled. If Dylan hadn't had his hands full, he'd probably have grabbed her.

A protesting squeak issued from the baby's lips.

"Uh-oh." Laura stood cautiously. "I think she's about to lose patience with us."

Squeaks turned into little bleats that made Jessica smile. "When's she gonna learn how to talk?" she wanted to know. "When's she gonna learn how to play Barbies? When's she gonna learn to walk?"

"Not for a couple of days at the earliest," her father teased. "Come on, let's help Mom get settled into bed so she can feed K.C. before she gets really worked up." He took the baby from Dylan, who resisted the urge to hang onto her. "You two are welcome to stay, but this may take a while. Then I think Laura needs to get some rest."

"I am a little worn-out," Laura admitted. "But I want to thank you both so much for coming. Please come again, any time you want to."

"We'll do that, but now I think it's time we were leaving." Katy glanced at Dylan and he nodded agreement. "Is there anything we can do for you before we go? Anything at all?"

"Can't think of a thing."

"Then we'll see you soon."

Katy led the way out the front door, halting on the porch. She turned on Dylan so unexpectedly that he took a step back.

"Come to my house for dinner tomorrow night," she said.

What was she up to now? "Why?" he asked, suspicious.

"I—" She stopped, drew in a deep breath, pursed her lips and then the words spilled out, "—want to

find out who you are and what you did with the Dylan
I've known all my life.''

"Cute," he said. "What's it mean?"

"It *means*," she said, punching up the word, "that
I've actually been...kind of almost liking you the last
couple of days."

"Restrain your enthusiasm, if you can," he suggested dryly.

She turned red. He enjoyed it.

"Dylan, it's hard enough to admit I don't detest
you at this particular moment. Don't rub it in, okay?"

"Okay."

"So you'll be there?"

"I dunno. I've been in town more than I've been
at the ranch the last couple of days. My cows are
gonna think I died and everybody forgot to tell 'em.''

"That's why you hire a passel of ornery cowboys,"
she pointed out sweetly. "Yes or no, it's all the same
to me."

He grimaced. "There you go again, boosting my
self esteem." He hopped down off the porch. "Sure,
I'll be there. Make it worth my time by going to lots
of trouble. And in case you don't know, I'm a meat-
and-potatoes kind of guy."

"Ohh, Dylan Cole!" She clenched her fists and
glared at him. "You make me so mad I could sock
you and then..." all the starch flowed out of her.
"And then," she said, "I see you holding a baby as
if it were the most precious thing on earth and I
think...I wonder...if there might be hope for you
yet."

He shrugged, keeping his face carefully impassive.

Walking to his pickup, he drove away...not because her words meant nothing to him but because they meant too much.

By the time Dylan knocked on her door the following evening, Katy was a nervous wreck. How could she deal with Dylan as if he were just anyone? Their history was too long, their differences too deep. Why was she doing this to herself? It would never work and she knew it.

But she had to try, she bolstered her flagging spirits. *She would be nice to him!* She wouldn't jump on every word he said, wouldn't try to keep one up on him, wouldn't look for hidden and dastardly meaning behind every word.

She would be just as nice and girly as she knew how to be. And she'd start by cooking meat and potatoes, even though that was *bor*-ing.

She opened her kitchen door with a smile on her face. Dylan stood there, grinning expectantly and holding out a handful of drooping wildflowers.

Hot words jumped to her lips: *Don't you know you shouldn't pick wildflowers? Think about the ecology! If you wanted to bring flowers, that's what florists are for—* Blah, blah, blah!

She swallowed hard and forced a smile. "For me?" She took the flowers, then stepped aside and gestured to him to enter.

He frowned. "You like the flowers, do you?"

"Of course." Waltzing to a cabinet, she extracted a vase and put the poor little things in water. The thing about wildflowers was, they lasted for such a short time once picked.

And yet, they *were* pretty—white and blue and orange.

She turned to him with a smile. "Would you care for a drink?"

"Sure. What you got?"

"Soft drinks, beer, wine."

"Beer," he said.

Where was the man's class? Where was his imagination?

She retrieved a beer from the depths of the refrigerator and poured it into a pilsner glass. When she offered it to him, he frowned.

"You're gettin' kinda fancy," he said, holding it as if he expected it to shatter in his hands.

"You *are* company," she countered lightly.

"Since when?"

"*Since*—" Too emphatic. She started over. "Since we agreed to spend time together. Work with me here, Dylan. I'm trying to find out if I can treat you the way I'd treat any..." She cast about for the proper word.

"Potential boyfriend?" he supplied.

She wanted to groan but didn't. "That's right," she said firmly. "I mean, do we bicker all the time simply out of habit? Could we treat each other with courtesy and respect if we tried?"

"I dunno," he said doubtfully. "Sounds kinda boring to me."

"Will you *try*?" Her resolve was already slipping. She had to calm down and stay calmed down, but when she was around him, her temper always seemed to soar.

"Do I *have* to?"

She refused to fall for his plaintive appeal. "I would appreciate it," she said with dignity.

"Okay, I suppose I can try." He hauled out a kitchen chair.

"Don't sit there!"

He leaped back. "Is it booby trapped?" He looked almost hopeful.

"Of course not. I just don't want to entertain you in the kitchen."

"Why not? I like kitchens. And I *don't* like being entertained, as you put it."

"Dylan, will you let me do this my way?" She faced him with hands on hips.

He rolled his eyes and said again, "Do I *have* to?"

She took a deep breath and counted to ten. Then she said, "Yes," very sweetly.

His sigh sounded resigned. "What do you want me to do?"

"Go into the living room and sit down. I'll bring in the hors d'oeuvres."

"You *are* getting fancy. Okay, it's your party."

She certainly hoped so, she told herself as she retrieved the tiny rolled sandwiches and shrimp spread from the refrigerator. She was going to be nice to Dylan tonight if it killed both of them.

Maybe then she'd know whether the feelings she'd been fighting to suppress were the real thing or just a figment of her imagination.

* * *

If there was anything Dylan hated, it was eating fancy food and drinking out of fancy glasses. But Katy seemed so intent upon what ever she was trying to prove that he did his best to go along with her.

"Would you care for another shrimp canapé?" she asked, offering the tray.

"Thirty is about my limit," he declined. Darned things tasted like fish glue but the new and nice Katy might take offense at such a comment.

She smiled; she looked bored.

He couldn't blame her. He was pretty damned bored himself with all this sweetness and light.

She settled back in her chair. "You were saying that the cattle are in good shape for the winter," she reminded him.

"Oh, yeah, the cattle." He sipped daintily at his beer, treating it as if it were wine in the tall flared glass. "Good thing, too. Judging by the fur on the critters I'm seeing, we're in for a long and early winter."

"But the weather's beautiful now," she protested politely. "A true Indian summer."

"What you gonna believe, me or your own eyes?"

A spark leaped in those eyes and was quickly extinguished. "I'll withhold judgment," she said.

He set his glass down with more force than necessary. "Since when? Katy, this new you—" An aroma of burning meat wafted past and he frowned.

"What is it?" she asked, still cool and contained.

"Were you planning to serve roast beef for dinner?"

"I'm *still* planning on it."

"I hope you've got a plan B because unless I'm mistaken, that roast is going up in smoke even as we speak."

Her smile was smug. "What in the world are you talking about? I'm using a method that never fails. I sear the meat under high heat and then I turn down the temperature and—" She stopped short and a look of total panic came across her face. She took a tentative sniff and jumped to her feet. "Oh, my goodness! What have I done?"

He followed her into the kitchen, glad that at least she'd dropped all that phony placidity. It didn't suit her at all.

The kitchen was free of smoke—until she opened the oven. Then enough smoke poured out to set them both to coughing.

Katy grabbed the roasting pan with oven mitts and set it on top of the stove, then snatched up a towel and started fanning the smoke toward the open back door. He joined in and soon the air was breathable again.

Dylan, who'd kind of enjoyed the excitement, turned back to find Katy slumped in a chair at the small kitchen table. She stared at the lump of charcoal in the roasting pan with disbelief on her face.

She looked at him. "I can't believe this is happening!"

"Yeah, well…" He leaned down to peer at the oven dial. "My guess is that 500 degrees probably is too hot for any extended period of time."

"Five hundred!" She leaned forward to see for herself. "But I swear I turned it back to three-fifty."

Her eyes narrowed. "You didn't happen to mess with my dial, did you?"

"Get outa here!" He looked at her incredulously. "I may be a low-life and all, but I rarely burn my own dinner on purpose."

"Okay, I apologize for that one. I know I...was a little distracted. Maybe I *did* just screw up."

"Hey," he said lightly, "it happens to everyone. I screwed up myself once, back about 1997."

She didn't laugh as he'd intended. Instead, tears spilled over onto her cheeks. "I wanted this to be perfect," she blurted. "I wanted to see if we could have a nice dinner and act like normal human beings just once in our lives." She turned her head away. "I see now that we can't."

"Normality is greatly overrated." He took her by the elbows and lifted her to her feet.

"Maybe so, but it's normal to feed someone when you invite them to dinner."

"To hell with dinner. We can go out to eat or we can have a bowl of cereal—I don't care. I didn't come for the food."

She grew very still. "Then why did you come?"

"Because you asked me, or rather, told me to. Because I seem to be spending a lot of time trying to please you these days."

"Please me?" She looked thoroughly confused. "But all you do is argue and annoy me."

"Yeah. Fun, isn't it?"

"No!" She threw out stiff arms, shaking away his light hold. "We act like a couple of kids when we're around each other."

''You could be right about that. Kids spend a lot of time trying to figure out what it is they're feeling, besides lust, of course. Isn't that what you've been trying to do tonight?''

''Not exactly...well, maybe sort of.'' She was breathing lightly, through slightly parted lips that looked soft as velvet. ''But it didn't work.''

''Because it was phony.'' He settled his hands at her waist. ''All that nicey-nice stuff isn't you, Katy.''

''Yes, it is! I can be nice—I *am* nice, around anyone but you. You bring out the worst in me, Dylan.''

''You bring out the best in me.''

''If that's the best—'' She stopped, biting her lip. ''See,'' she gave him an accusing look, ''you made me say that.''

''I encouraged you. I didn't make you.'' He gave a little yank and she stumbled into him, her hips flat against his, green eyes going wide.

''You...make me...crazy,'' she murmured. ''I don't like feeling crazy.''

''Do you like feeling this?'' He slid his hands up her sides until his thumbs nestled beneath the curve of her breasts. At the same time, he slipped one knee between her legs, which tightened around him almost imperceptibly.

''No,'' she said, and the word was little more than an expulsion of breath. ''This isn't right. Not with you, Dylan.''

He nuzzled her temple. ''Why not? We're practically engaged.''

''That...was a bad idea.''

''Kiss me and then say that.''

"If I kiss you...if I kiss you—oh, hell!"

Sliding her arms around his neck, she yanked his head down and planted her lips on his. He wanted to whoop and holler, it felt so good to have her take the initiative. Her mouth was sweet as nectar, her body pliable and seductive. He was already thinking thoughts of bedrooms and deserts when the telephone shrilled.

He didn't release her. "Don't answer it," he urged, nibbling at her ear.

"I've got to." Breathing hard, she managed to shove his hands aside and stagger to the telephone on the wall near the door. Her "Hello?" was barely audible.

Suddenly she straightened and shot a look over her shoulder at Dylan, who lounged against the table and tried to get control of himself. Every time he touched her, his composure slipped a little further, a little faster.

"Yes," she said in the phone. Her eyes widened. "Next weekend?" She swallowed hard. "Yes, I know when my birthday is but when you didn't mention it again, I thought maybe you'd forgotten...uh-huh. Uh-huh. All right, Grandma, I'll see all of you a week from today."

So the whole family was about to descend upon her for a birthday party. Tough on her, he supposed.

He tried to take her in his arms again.

"What are you *doing?*" She batted his hands away.

He frowned, thinking it should have been obvious. "Picking up where we left off."

"No way!" Turning her back, she walked to the sink, then faced him defiantly. "Practically my entire family will be here next weekend."

"Sure, I remember. For your birthday party." He followed her, slipping his hands around her waist.

She stepped aside. "Don't do that! I can't think when you do that."

"Okay, why don't we clear both our minds and then we can talk." Bending, he scooped her up in his arms.

For a moment she hung there with astonishment written all over her face. Then she stiffened. "What are you *doing?*"

"Moving this into the bedroom." He grinned. "That's where we were heading."

"Are you *crazy?* Put me down this instant!"

She wasn't kidding. He stood her on her feet and backed away. "What the hell's your problem, Katy? That's where this was heading and you damned well know it."

"I know no such thing!"

"Don't lie to either one of us. If that phone hadn't rung, we'd be—"

"We would not!" She shoved tousled hair out of her face.

"Sure, we would. That's why you invited me here tonight, because—"

"No! Stop it, Dylan." She turned her back to him and her words became muffled. "This isn't working."

He put his hands on her shoulders and felt her tremble. "What isn't?"

"This stupid arrangement we made. It was all right until—"

"Until what?" He brushed her hair behind her ear.

"Until K.C. Being a part of that…sharing it…has made everything different."

"Different better."

"Different worse!" She whirled away from him. "I can't go on with this, not even for Grandma."

He was beginning to get the drift of her intentions, despite efforts not to. "Spell it out," he grated.

She took a deep breath. "Our deal's off," she said. "No more dates, no more pretending. You'll have to find another way to keep all your admirers off your back."

Aching all over, he gave her a glacial stare. "Then you'll have to find some other way to keep your grandmother from kicking off when she finds out you have no intentions of giving her what she wants—a grandson-in-law and great-grandkids."

"That's cold," she accused.

"*Saying* it is cold? Not near as cold as doing it."

For a full minute, they glared at each other. Then Dylan drew a disgusted breath. "That's it, then."

"I'm afraid so."

"In that case, I may as well go home to my cows and stay there."

Turning, he strode out of her kitchen—and her life, he devoutly hoped.

CHAPTER EIGHT

KATY HAD A busy week at work—the Rawhide Chamber of Commerce had gotten its act together and she must dutifully report the story. She didn't get a chance to drop by to visit the baby until Friday after work—at least, she told herself she was visiting the baby. Actually she needed to vent, and Laura was the only one who would understand.

Once at the Reynolds' house, however, she found it hard to find an opening when there was so much cooing and gooing to be done.

This time she made no protest when Laura placed the precious bundle in her arms. Holding the sweet-smelling baby, Katy buried her nose in the curve of the little shoulder.

"Want one?" Laura asked with a smile. "They're easy to get."

Katy groaned. "Maybe for you. For me, we're talking impossible."

"The best way is to get married," Laura advised, straight-faced. "Of course, that's not the *only* way but it's the one I recommend."

"Ain't gonna happen."

"Maybe not tomorrow, but someday."

"Maybe never." Katy couldn't put a good face on it, even for her best friend

Laura looked alarmed. "But I thought there was

hope for you and Dylan, since you're getting along much better. Matt and I talked about it and we were hoping maybe you two might really end up being perfect for each other.''

Katy concentrated on smoothing the dark fluff on K.C.'s head. ''That's over.''

''What do you mean, *over?* Didn't you say your grandmother is coming Saturday?''

''Yes.'' Filled with despair, Katy finally looked up. ''But Saturday night...things almost got out of hand between me and Dylan. So we've called it off.''

''Out of hand...?'' Laura cocked a brow. ''I take it that means you almost went to bed with him.''

''Laura! I didn't say that.''

''But you meant it.''

''Well...yes.'' Katy squeezed her eyes closed. ''Oh, it's so complicated and confusing! The only time I feel comfortable around the man is when we're fighting.''

''That's the only time you don't have to confront the attraction between you—now, don't deny it. It's obvious to the most casual observer.''

''It is?'' Dumfounded, Katy stared at her friend.

''After all the years the two of you have made public spectacles of your quarrels, why do you think people have been so willing to accept you as a couple?''

''Because they'll believe anything?''

''No! Because there's always been this underlying tension...a kind of sexual tension.''

Katy groaned. ''I don't want to hear this.''

''Perhaps you *need* to hear it. I'm not trying to make matters worse, Katy, really I'm not, but if there's a chance for you and Dylan you should grab it.''

"No chance at all.'' Katy's stomach clenched when she said it. "Look, I don't want to talk about Dylan anymore. It's over and that's that. Let's change the subject.'' She stroked K.C.'s cheek. "I'll bet it'll be hard for you when you have to leave this angel and come back to work.''

"About that…''

Katy looked up sharply. "Laura, please don't tell me you're not coming back.''

Laura looked apologetic. "I'm sorry. I just don't see any way I can go back to work when my maternity leave is up. I've pretty much decided to stay home until she starts school.''

Katy felt sick. Everything was changing. Her old adversarial relationship with Dylan was at an impasse, her best friend wouldn't be coming back to work, Katy herself was probably going to give her grandmother a heart attack—

For a moment she stared sightlessly through the window, belatedly focusing on…snowflakes?

October 23 and it was *snowing?*

Somehow, she thought, a fitting metaphor for my life, which is also bleak and out of control.

When Dylan realized he'd have to come into town early Saturday morning for supplies, he called Matt to meet him for coffee at the Rawhide Café. Matt arrived with Zach in tow.

Matt pulled out a chair for the boy. "I'm taking my son to the hardware store after we leave here,'' he said with pride. "A kid can't start learning about hammers and saws any too early."

"Guess not," Dylan agreed around an unexpected tightening in his chest. Damn, he envied Matt! He reached out to ruffle the boy's hair and a grinning Zach evaded the hand. Dylan laughed. "I wouldn't mind having a great little kid like Zach," he admitted.

"There's an easy way to do it," Matt pointed out. "First you find a wife and then you go to work on the problem. I might add, it's nice work, if you can get it."

"Yeah." Dylan felt uncomfortable agreeing, after what had happened last weekend with Katy, whom he hadn't seen since. He'd been perfectly willing to get in a little baby-making practice until she'd all but spit in his eye.

"Uh-oh." Matt glanced significantly at the boy who was taking in every word. "Does that mean you and Katy are having problems?"

"When haven't we had problems?"

"Good point. Uh…Zach?"

"Yes, Daddy?"

"You're always asking if you can sit on the stools at the counter. There aren't too many people here today so I don't think it would bother anyone if you gave it a shot."

"Goody!" The boy jumped up.

"Just don't fall off," Matt warned. "You've already lost enough teeth."

Zach grinned broadly and for the first time, Dylan realized the boy was missing his two front teeth.

"Way to go, Zach!" Dylan gave him a high five.

"Did your dad come up with some bucks for those teeth?"

"The tooth fairy did!" Zach turned and trotted across the room to the counter with the swiveling stools before it.

For a minute, the two men remained silent. Then Matt returned to the subject at hand. "I kinda thought K.C.'s birth was bringing the two of you closer together."

"Yeah." Dylan shrugged and looked away. "I thought so, anyway. But last time I was at her house we both...got pretty worked up. Then she just turned it off, told me the whole deal was over and that was that."

"You have no idea what made her do that?"

Dylan wished Matt wouldn't look at him with so much speculation in his eyes. No way did he intend to tell even his best buddy that the real issue had been sex.

Although Matt probably guessed.

So Dylan copped out. "Why does a woman do anything? She told me to hit the road so I did, end of story."

"Damned shame." Matt signaled to the waitress for coffee. "I know this started out as a sham but you two coulda been good together."

"Yeah, sure, like oil and water."

"Like apple pie and ice cream."

"Like sheep and coyotes."

"I was thinking more like Kate and what's-his-name in *The Taming of the Shrew*."

Dylan recoiled. "Katy's a pain in the butt most of the time, but I wouldn't call her a shrew."

"Defending her, huh?" Matt chuckled. "You may *think* you're through with her, but trust me on this—you're not."

Which, Dylan thought, just went to show that Matt didn't know everything, even if he thought he did.

By the time the Andrews' family van pulled into the driveway Saturday afternoon, Katy was pacing the floor and looking out the window every two minutes. What she was going to do Sunday when her family expected Dylan for ice cream and birthday cake, she had no idea. Perhaps by then, she'd have found a way to break the bad news to her grandmother...gently.

Squaring her shoulders and taking a deep breath, she went out to meet her visitors through the light flurry of snowflakes that had begun only minutes earlier.

Her mother was first out of the van, which had been driven by Mack. She came forward with arms outstretched.

"Do you believe this weather!" she exclaimed, hugging her daughter. "All the way up from Denver, I kept remembering why we moved down in the first place."

Katy returned the hug. "Don't worry, it won't amount to anything," she said. "Even for Colorado, this is a bit early for a major storm." She turned toward the van from which her grandmother was emerging, assisted by Josh.

"Grandma!" she exclaimed, opening her arms.

Josh pressed a cane into Grandma's hand and Katy stopped short. "What's happened? You weren't using a cane when I saw you at the family reunion."

"It's nothing." To prove it, Granny waved the cane in the air. "I've just got a hitch in my get-along." She looked around with quick, anxious concern. "Where's that handsome fella of yours, Katy? I've been looking forward to giving him a big hug!"

"Give it to me instead, Granny." Over her grand-mother's shoulder, Katy's gaze met her brother's. He frowned, a question in his eyes. She made a face that was supposed to say, "I'll explain later!" and kept on hugging her grandma.

Katy's little two-bedroom house really wasn't big enough for five people, but the Andrews were a hardy clan and making do was not a big problem. She installed her mother and grandmother in her bedroom, moved herself into the smaller second bedroom which she normally used as an office, and the boys would sleep in the living room, one on the sofa and the other on the floor.

Knowing that in advance, they'd even brought a sleeping bag. It would be all right, she assured herself—although still somewhat anxiously. They'd probably be tripping over each other a lot but it wouldn't be the first time.

While Granny and Mother unpacked, the boys cornered Katy in the kitchen.

"Okay," Mack said, "where is he?"

It seemed pointless to reply, "Who?" Katy gritted

her teeth. "God only knows," she said shortly. "I don't."

The boys stared at her, mouths agape. Josh recovered first.

"You've had a lovers' quarrel," he guessed.

"Since we were never lovers, that would be a stretch."

"You've had a little misunderstanding," Mack took his shot at mind-reading.

"It wasn't little and it wasn't a misunderstanding. It was a full-blown, out-and-out, no-holds-barred disagreement. We're finished."

Mack groaned. "How could you do this to us?"

"To you?"

"Okay, to Grandma—but us, too. How fed up do you think we are of hearing her and Mom carrying on night and day about our old-maid sister? It's enough to make a man sick."

"Well, gee, fellas, that's a good reason for a girl to get married." Katy knew her voice dripped sarcasm, but by this time didn't care.

"You got everybody's hopes up," Josh accused. "You shouldn't have said anything until you were sure."

Mack added ominously, "This could kill Grandma."

"Don't exaggerate!" Katy swung on them. "I'm doing my best to keep Grandma alive. I don't need my brothers telling me how I've messed up. I *know* I've messed up, but I'm doing the best I can."

"Please," Josh said, "don't cry! Can it be fixed?"

"Can what be fixed?" she snuffled.

"You and Dylan, what else?"

"No. No, it can't, and I don't want you two sticking your noses into it."

"At least tell us what happened." Mack's eyes narrowed and for a moment, he looked like a stranger.

A big, strong, dangerous stranger.

Josh chimed in. "If he did anything to hurt our big sister, we're prepared to beat the sh—stuffing out of him. Just tell us how bad he did you so we know how bad to do him."

"Joshua Andrews!" Katy grabbed him by both shirt lapels. "If you harm one hair on that man's head, I swear I'll kill you! Do you clearly understand what I am telling you?"

Josh looked past her and she supposed he was communicating with his brothers as much as with her. "Sure, Katy," he said in a soothing voice. "I know what you're telling me—that you still love the bum."

"That's not it at all. I don't love him, I never loved him—"

But she was shouting at thin air; her brothers had thrown open the back door and dived out into the few flakes still falling.

Dylan had no damned business going to the Painted Pony Saloon Saturday afternoon, but he was in too bad a mood to stay home alone.

When one of his hands invited him along, he shrugged and said, "Why the hell not?"

Now he stood at the bar with a beer in his hand and blackness in his heart.

What was the matter with the woman, anyway—

and why couldn't he stop thinking about her? He hadn't suggested anything she hadn't thought of herself. Katy Andrews might be a major pain, but she wasn't stupid. She knew what this new and exasperating pull between them was, as well as he did.

What did she think, that he liked this new state of affairs? He *didn't* like it! He didn't like being tied up into knots by a woman he'd spent his life disliking. Fighting with. Needling. Fending off.

Whatever: he just plain didn't like it.

"Gimme another beer, barkeep." He held up his empty mug. *She* served beer in fancy glasses. Sheesh! "Barkeep!" He banged his mug on the bar. "Another beer here."

Hands closed over his arms from both sides and a voice said, "Skip it, barkeep. The gentleman's got business elsewhere at the moment."

Then those damned big Andrews boys picked him up off his feet and more or less carried him over to a table, where they deposited him none too gently.

Josh and Mack sat down on either side of him. They did not look friendly.

Dylan glared back, more as a matter of form than anything else. They were as alike as two peas in a pod: big, broad-shouldered, square-jawed, with short-clipped hair. They moved with a confidence that bespoke athletic backgrounds.

Mack—or was it Josh?—leaned forward and spoke in a low but serious voice. "We hear you and our sister have split up."

"Pretty much."

The brothers exchanged narrow-eyed glances. ''That's what she said, but we didn't believe her.''

''Believe her.''

Josh cocked his head. ''Is something wrong with you?''

''Not a damned thing!'' Dylan sputtered.

''Something wrong with our sister?''

''I never got close enough to find out.''

''That's good. If you're gonna love her and leave her, I'd just as soon you never—''

''I didn't love her and leave her. I never had any intentions of loving her and leaving her.'' That was true. Love had never entered into the equation.

''Then what happened?''

Dylan considered. ''You're aware that Katy and I have known each other practically our entire lives, right?''

Two heads nodded simultaneously.

''Then maybe you also know that we never got along very well.'' He added hastily, ''Until recently, that is.''

Again the duplicate nods.

''Hey, no one was more surprised than we were to realize…to realize…?'' What the hell had they realized? That a long-simmering sexual attraction lurked just beneath the surface? That it was just waiting to bust loose?

The brothers were waiting patiently.

Dylan grimaced. ''Katy's a great girl but she threw me out on my—she gave me my walking papers. It wasn't *my* idea.'' Self-righteous indignation felt good, real good.

"What if she changed her mind?" Mack wanted to know.

"She won't," Dylan said with finality.

"But what if she did?"

"Well..." What *would* he do?

Across the barroom, he saw a woman enter clinging to the arm of a tall man he'd never seen before. Brandee Haycox. He'd only got into this mess because he'd wanted to turn her down gently. He hadn't bargained for anything that had come after.

Anything like the emotional upheaval of K.C.'s birth, or the frightening changes in his feelings toward Katy.

But with her brothers staring at him with unblinking attention, Dylan shrugged and said, "If she changed her mind, I'd welcome her back with open arms."

"You mean it?"

"Hell, yes. But it'll never happen."

"Don't be too sure." Both men seemed to relax.

Josh grinned. "Welcome back to the family," he said. "I figured it was only a misunderstanding."

"Yeah," Mack agreed, "and a good thing, too. Grandma's in no shape to take any bad news. You and Katy breaking up would be the worst news she could get."

Dylan liked Grandma Andrews. He even liked these two big galoots. "Can I buy you a beer?" he asked.

"Naw, we need to get back and tell Katy it's up to her." The big men stood. "We appreciate your honesty, Dylan. If we ever thought you were lying to us—"

The other brother pounded a fist into the palm of his hand, smiling. "It won't come to that," he said confidently. "We'll see you at the birthday party tomorrow, *brother*."

"Yeah, *brother*."

They turned and marched out of the bar. Dylan sat at his table alone, wondering what on earn those two were going to do if they ever learned the truth.

They weren't going to learn it from him. Let Katy stand up to their heavy-handed methods. She would, too. No way would she come to him and ask him to pretend they were a happy couple again.

If she did, though, he'd be in a world of hurt.

A woman's laughter floated through the crowded bar. Brandee, over at a table in the corner with that new guy. It'd been a long time since he'd seen her and she didn't look half-bad to a man with a bruised ego.

Yeah, she was too aggressive and she'd already been married and divorced a couple of times, and her daddy tended to get real ugly with those who messed with her, but at least if Dylan gave in and hooked up with her, Katy wouldn't come near him. Besides, Brandee had chased him off and on since high school. Maybe it was time to let her catch him.

Dylan stood and hitched up his Wranglers. With determined steps, he made his way to Brandee's table. She looked up in surprise, a smile spreading over her face.

"Okay, Brandee," he said, "you win. Take me! I'm yours!" And he flung wide his arms.

The smile froze on her face. "Uhh...too late," she

said, obviously embarrassed. "Dylan, I'd like you to meet my husband, Basil. Basil, this is Dylan Cole, an...uhh...old friend."

Katy almost welcomed the return of her brothers, even knowing they would start in on her again about Dylan. Mom and Granny were stuck on the same groove and it was getting harder and harder to be evasive.

She had to tell them the truth, but how? What could she possibly say that wouldn't prove traumatic, or worse?

Mack wasted no time in dragging her out into the kitchen. "We just talked to Dylan," he announced in a melodramatic whisper.

Katy groaned. "Will you guys butt out? My love life is none of your business."

"What love life?" Mack grimaced. "Maybe that's why you snapped. Women have needs, you know. Men take all the heat on that subject but women have—"

"I don't need my brother to tell me about women!" She glared at him.

"Sugar, you need all the help you can get," he said earnestly. "Dylan is sorry and wants to make up."

"He didn't say that!"

"Almost. He said the break-up was your idea." He cocked his head. "Is that right?"

"Well...yes. But he—"

"I don't want to hear any rationalizations. I just

want you to hop on over to the Painted Pony and tell the man you were wrong and you want him back.''

"But I *wasn't* wrong and I *don't*—" She stopped, chewing her lower lip.

"Can't say it, can you?" He nodded his head wisely. "You *do* want him back—admit it. He wants you back, too—and this time, let nature take its course?"

He gave her a knowing stare and left her standing there in front of the sink, wondering what he and Josh had said and done to Dylan, and vice versa. Whatever it was apparently hadn't resulted in bloodshed, which was a relief.

"Katy? Katy, dear, we must discuss your party."

"In a minute, Mom."

Should she take a chance and go to the Painted Pony? *Was* he waiting for her to come to him?

She wanted to! Her heart beat faster at that realization. She missed him terribly; she even missed their fights. Did he miss her—and them—too?

Grabbing her jacket from the hook near the back door, she strode into the living room, pulling it on. "Mom, Granny, I've got to go out for a few minutes. I won't be long, I promise."

"But your party!"

"Let her go, Mom," Josh advised. He added softly, "I'll tell you what's going on later."

Katy just bet he would.

The Painted Pony was crowded so she didn't see him right away. It took two complete turns of the room before she realized he simply wasn't there. Frowning, she stood in the middle of the room and considered her options.

That's when she saw Brandee Haycox, alone at a table. If he'd been here, she would know.

Working her way through, Katy slipped into an empty seat across from Brandee. "Hi," she said. "Have you seen Dylan here tonight?"

"Sure have." Brandee looked amused.

"Did he leave?"

"I'm not sure. Probably."

"You spoke to him?"

"That's right."

"Brandee," Katy said in exasperation, "it's like pulling teeth to get anything out of you tonight."

"Sorry. I was just curious to see how you'd handle this."

"Handle what?"

Brandee shrugged. "Obviously, you and Dylan are having problems. I was curious to see how you were going to approach me."

"Now you know," Katy said shortly. She couldn't help looking around, still hoping she'd see him because no way was she going to drive all the way to his ranch in a potential snowstorm.

"After the way he went to bat for you with my father, I figured you'd give the man a little more slack," Brandee said.

Katy's head snapped around. "What are you talking about?"

Brandee's blue eyes went wide. "You don't know? I'm talking about that hatchet job you did on the Chamber of Commerce a while back."

"I have never done a hatchet job in my life," Katy said. "Of course, any story that isn't one hundred percent favorable is always *called* a hatchet job, even when it isn't."

"Whatever." Brandee shrugged. "That's what Daddy called it, anyway. So he went to Dylan all in a huff and told him to call you off. Dylan stood right up for you, though. He actually told Daddy not to run around town bad-mouthing you."

Katy stared at the other woman, big-eyed. "He did?"

Brandee nodded emphatically. "And Daddy said, 'Are you threatening violence?' and Dylan said, 'Hell no! I'm promising retribution!'"

"Were you there?" Katy could hardly believe her ears. Dylan needed to keep on the right side of Banker Haycox.

Brandee laughed. "No, but Daddy gave me a blow-by-blow description. He was really shocked that Dylan would talk to him that way. But when he cooled down, I think he got a kick out of it."

"That's a relief." It was, too. She hadn't wanted her work to cause problems for Dylan.

"Daddy got in his licks, too."

"He did?"

"He said he told Dylan that it was easy to see who wore the pants in *that* relationship and Dylan laughed. He said you were a match for any man, including him."

Katy felt almost dizzy with surprise and pleasure. She'd had no idea that anything like this had happened, and she felt a warm glow hearing about it.

"You know," Brandee said in a musing tone, "you and me and Dylan go way back. I never would have believed you guys as a couple in a million years, if Daddy hadn't told me about that. I guess it must be love."

Was it? Katy swallowed hard. "Thanks for telling me, Brandee. I had no idea. I'm actually a little surprised you'd...you know, be so candid about it."

"With reason. I probably wouldn't have said anything except when I saw Dylan earlier, he was in pretty bad shape, plus—here comes my *real* reason now." She smiled at the tall man who'd just approached the table. "Basil, I'd like you to meet Katy Andrews. Katy, this is my husband Basil."

Brandee was married.

Dylan's reasons for cooperating in the first place had just flown out the window.

CHAPTER NINE

BREAKFAST SUNDAY MORNING was a family affair with Grandma, Katy and her brothers all clustered around the small kitchen table while Mom fried eggs and flipped pancakes. It gave Katy a warm feeling to have them all here for her birthday, even under somewhat false pretenses.

She'd figured out how she was going to handle the "Dylan situation," however. After lying awake most of the night worrying the problem over, she'd concluded that there was only one thing to do.

She would grovel.

She would drive out to the Bear Claw Ranch right after breakfast and throw herself on Dylan's mercy, if any. Surely he'd spend one more day pretending for the sake of a nice little old lady like Granny.

After the interrogations of yesterday, no one seemed willing to even mention Dylan's name this morning.

Josh shoved away his empty plate and patted his stomach. "Ma, you make the greatest pancakes in the world."

"Why, thank you, son. I try to please." When Liz smiled, a dimple appeared in her cheek. "Mother, is something wrong with your breakfast?"

Grandma, who'd hardly eaten a bite, shook her

head. "I'm too excited to eat," she said. "I do love parties." She turned to Katy. "It won't be big or anything. We just invited the Reynolds family, and of course—" Granny stopped speaking and her eyes went wide. "Oops. We weren't supposed to mention *him*."

"Why not?" Katy laughed nervously. "I guess it's time I came clean with all of you."

Four heads nodded agreement.

"Dylan and I had a fight."

Liz clucked like a mother hen. "That's what we all figured, dear. Are you going to make up in time for the party?"

"I certainly hope so."

Mack leaned forward. "See, she went over to the Painted Pony last night because Josh and I told her Dylan was there, but he left before she could talk to him."

"Too bad," Liz sympathized. "Of course, you can always just call him on the phone."

"This is something that needs to be done face to face," Katy said. "I thought maybe after breakfast I could drive out to the ranch and talk to him there."

"The party's not until two," Granny inserted. "That's plenty of time to get back."

Katy nodded. "Of course. Although there's always the chance that he won't want to…uh, pick up where we left off."

"Pshaw!" Granny scoffed. "Of course he will. What young man would hold a grudge when his sweetie comes to him all contrite?"

Katy had to laugh, even if somewhat ruefully. For all she knew, Dylan would throw her out.

Or maybe not...

It was snowing lightly when she drove out of town shortly after ten. Several inches of uncharacteristically wet snow had already collected but she doubted it was going to amount to much more than that.

But as she drove deeper into the mountains she began to wonder. It was snowing much harder here, although visibility remained reasonably good and there was little traffic to impede her progress.

Once she turned off the highway, it seemed as if she'd also turned into a break in the weather. With a brightening sky ahead, she could relax a little. Although snow had already piled up in places, she wasn't really worried.

Of course, by then the only thing that *really* worried her was how Dylan was going to react to seeing her here. She'd only been to the ranch a few times, and always for school events—his folks had enjoyed hosting barbecues and picnics and hayrides for the youth of Rawhide. After his father died and his mother moved to Florida, Dylan had taken on sole responsibility for the ranch and there'd been no reason for Katy to come.

Was he even here? Heart in her throat, she drove into the front yard of the massive log house. A single man must rattle around in there something fierce, she thought.

And smiled.

Braking, she jumped out, pulling her jacket closer. It wasn't really all that cold, although the wind was rising. She'd better say her piece and get out of here before more bad weather moved in.

Head down, she dashed for the house. When she reached the steps and looked up, he was standing in the open door watching her. She stopped short, surprised and uncertain.

"You're here," he said without smiling. "Come on in out of the weather."

Suddenly shy, she walked into a large entryway with hooks on the walls for coats. He took hers and hung it up while she stamped snow off her hiking boots.

She gave him a hesitant smile. "Do you believe this weather?"

"I'll believe most anything if someone can give me even a half-good reason why I should."

She frowned. "Is that supposed to mean something?"

He shrugged. "Come on in and get warm. I've got a fire going and a fresh pot of coffee."

The warmth of the great room embraced her. Walking to the massive stone fireplace, she extended her hands and looked around to admire the high ceilings and open beams.

"This is wonderful," she said.

He shrugged. "It works for me. Look, I've got a fresh pot of coffee."

She turned, savoring the heat of crackling logs on the backs of her legs. "Did you know I was coming?" she asked lightly.

"No." He did not look amused.

She waited, thinking that she'd probably made a terrible mistake coming here. When she had a mug of steaming coffee between trembling hands, she tried to think of a way to begin.

Crossing to the big leather couch, he sat down and reached for his own mug on the rough-hewn table. "What brings you out on a day like this, as if I didn't know?"

She took a deep breath. "Uh…my family's here."

"I saw your brothers last night."

"Were they…too bad?"

He shrugged. "What did they tell you?"

"That…that all you wanted was for me to ask you to come back." She peered at him intently, hating the seriousness she saw in his face. "How close is that to what really happened?"

"It's within shouting distance. But what they probably didn't tell you was that if I'd said anything else, they were fully prepared to…show me the error of my ways."

She groaned. "I'm sorry."

"It's not your fault. I could have told them the truth, but I thought you ought to do that."

She stood there for a long time, thinking about that. Then she said, "I'd like to tell the truth but I…I can't. Not yet."

"Because…?"

"Because of Granny—and Mother, too." She squared her shoulders and looked him right in the eye. "I'm sure you know why I'm here."

He met her gaze, his own just as level and perhaps equally determined. "Spell it out."

She swallowed hard. "I want you to come to my birthday party this afternoon. I want you to act as if we've made up our differences. If you will, I *promise* I'll find a way to tell them the truth...soon." She squeezed her eyes shut in her effort to convince him.

"And the truth is...?"

"That we aren't really a couple, that we put together this charade to give ourselves a little space."

"And then things happened, and *one* of us got scared and screwed it all up." He rose to stand before the sofa, tall and impressive and in complete control.

Katy looked away. "All right. You want me to admit it—I will! I did get scared because—" *Because I wanted to sleep with you more than anything in the world but I don't go around crawling into bed just for recreation.* "—because it was *you*, Dylan. Because I've known you too long and fought with you too hard and distrusted you too much. Oh, everything's all tangled up." She spun away from him.

"It sure as hell is."

"Will you do it or won't you?"

"I won't."

"Even if I beg?"

"You're not going to beg, Katy. You don't have it in you."

"Maybe not." Her voice felt gravelly. "May I ask why?"

"It's like you said— I've known you too long and fought with you too hard and distrusted you too much. Plus, I think you're wrong."

"Wrong?" She couldn't resist turning back so she could see his expression.

It was bleak.

"Wrong to drag this out any longer. In retrospect, we were wrong to even try to live a lie. It just can't be done."

"It could if we—oh, never mind." She stomped toward the entryway.

He followed. "Go ahead, say it."

"You won't help me because you've no longer got anything at risk."

"What's that supposed to mean?"

She grabbed her leather hat and slammed it on her head. "I saw Brandee last night—and met her husband."

"You went to the Painted Pony to talk to me?" He looked surprised.

"That's right."

"And now you think I'm being selfish, that I won't help you because my own problem has disappeared?"

"Well?" She shoved her arms through the sleeves of her heavy jacket. "Isn't that the truth?"

He looked thoughtful. "I didn't think so, but maybe it is."

"Dylan Cole, you're a rat!" She faced him with blazing eyes, arms stiff and hands clenched. "If my grandmother drops dead at the news—" She stared at him, appalled at what she'd been about to say, then continued more slowly. "—if she does, it'll be all my fault because I've never been able to find a guy...to find a guy I...could love."

Until now. She could love Dylan; she *did* love Dylan.

Turning, she plunged through the doorway and into a stinging snowstorm. Damn him for letting her think he could care...and for making her care.

Dylan stood at the window watching her struggle toward her vehicle. He felt completely numb from the encounter.

He'd turned her down, but he hadn't dared do otherwise. There was more at stake than she could imagine.

He said a short Anglo-Saxon word with deep feeling and turned away, then turned back again to watch her drive slowly out of the yard. When had he begun to care for her in this way that clenched his guts into knots and made him want to grab her and keep her here safe in his arms...forever?

He couldn't go back to Rawhide and put on an act for her family, because for him, it wasn't an act at all. It was reality. Incredible as it seemed, he'd fallen for little Katy Andrews. He hated to admit that—hated it like hell.

Her car fishtailed and he caught his breath. She held it in the turn and the red taillights were quickly swallowed up in the rapidly falling snow.

And all of a sudden, he snapped out of it. The weather was rotten and he'd let her drive out of here in a car that was completely inadequate for the conditions. What had he been thinking?

That he probably loved her?

He knew the road she traveled as well as he knew

the stairs leading up to his own bedroom. Right now she'd be on a stretch of road that wouldn't be too troublesome but at the bottom of the grade, a sharp right turn might very well send her slipping and sliding into the ditch.

He had to get to her before anything happened to her. As slowly as she'd have to drive, he'd make better time cutting across country on horseback than following her in the Jeep.

Dashing through the house, he laid his plans. He'd follow her as far as the highway; if she made it there, she'd be all right. He'd take the big black horse, Chief, because he was good in snow and strong as an ox.

At the back door he ripped his sheepskin-lined jacket off the hook and shoved his arms into it. If anything happened to her, he'd never be able to forgive himself.

Hell, he'd never get the chance because her brothers would kill him.

Blinded by tears, Katy rolled to a stop in the middle of the road. There was no need to pull over because hers was probably the only vehicle within ten miles of this spot.

Dashing at damp cheeks with cold hands, she relied on anger to overwhelm the hurt and humiliation. Damned weather. Damned car.

Damned birthday party.

Thirty-one today with no prospects for matrimony. Maybe Laura would let her borrow K.C. from time to time.

Calmer now, she peered through the windshield, past the arching wipers. The snow fell steadily, great fat flakes that quickly piled up. She was going to be lucky if she got out of here with both herself and her car in one piece.

Taking a deep breath to steady herself, she eased forward. The tires slipped briefly, then caught. She relaxed a little. If she was just careful, drove slowly, she'd make it. Of course, once she got home she still had to tell Granny...

The back tires slipped to the right and she corrected with the steering wheel. Heart in her throat, she skidded a few feet before she felt traction. There, that was all right, she rallied herself. She could handle this. All she had to do was be very, very careful—

A deer bounded into the middle of the road and paused, head held high. It was a magnificent sight which Katy was in no position to enjoy. She instinctively yanked the wheel to the left to avoid hitting the beautiful animal.

The deer bounded away, and the car plunged straight into a shallow ditch, coming to rest nosed into a pine tree. The engine continued to run, the snow continued to fall, and Katy continued to sit there in a state of shock.

Then she pulled herself together and shifted the vehicle into reverse, applying the lightest of pressure to the accelerator. Wheels spun but nothing else moved.

It didn't take a rocket scientist to realize that this car might not be moving under its own power until the spring thaw.

*   *   *

Dylan rode across country, the big black horse moving easily beneath him. He could barely see through the driving snow, but, with a complete knowledge of the country, he wasn't worried about himself.

He *was* worried about Katy, worried sick. How he could have let her walk out that way was beyond understanding. Even the fact that he'd been in a deep funk didn't excuse him, not for a minute.

He pulled his mount up on a ridge and looked around. He was right in the middle of the Rocky Mountains and couldn't see a mountain anywhere through this mess. He frowned. The road lay nearby and the question was, should he turn right toward town or left toward the ranch house?

He'd turn right, he decided, nudging the horse into movement again. Unless she was already stuck, she'd be further along than this. He could cut across the road and over a hill and—

He yanked back on the reins and peered through the white flakes. Something had caught his eye, something…red, and there it was again. Even as he watched, snow obscured the scene.

Turning the horse, he loped into the wind. Without sight to guide him, he went by guess and by golly. But his instincts were good and soon the shadow of a car loomed before him—a red car, Katy's car.

It was in a ditch, snow already beginning to pile up on the hood. All the lights were turned off and the engine was dead.

Stepping off the horse, he ran to the door and yanked it open. Nothing. She wasn't there. Dammit!

He peered around, trying to figure out what had happened and why she'd leave the car. Anyone who had a lick of sense knew that in a situation like this, you stayed with your vehicle and waited for someone to rescue you.

Only she hadn't. Swearing, he checked the ground in an attempt to figure out which way she'd gone—and found her tracks, already filling with snow. She'd headed toward the ranch at least. Assuming she didn't wander off the road, which would be real easy to do, he'd find her quickly and she'd be all right—once she survived the tongue-lashing she'd earned. If he didn't find her quickly—

He leaped back into the saddle and dug in his heels.

One minute Katy was stumbling through snow drifts, and the next she was snatched up before the saddle of some ghost rider she didn't even know was on her trail. Dylan, of course, but for a minute she was content to simply bury her face against his leather jacket and breathe a sigh of relief.

He didn't intend to waste his breath on words, she was happy to discover. Holding her tight against his chest, he sent his horse plunging ahead. Safe and confident of remaining so, she clung to him. She hadn't been in serious danger, of course, but there was definitely something scary about being alone in the middle of nowhere during a Colorado blizzard.

Unexpectedly soon, he yanked her upright. He had to lean close to be heard over the wind. "We're here," he yelled, pointing to the house barely visible through the snow. "Go upstairs to find something dry to put on. I'll be in as soon as I take care of the horse."

She nodded. He lifted her away from the saddle, dropping her to her feet practically on the doorstep. Head down, she struggled to the door and inside. The sudden warmth shocked her and she fought her way out of hat and coat, then unlaced her hiking boots and pulled them off. In stocking feet, she crossed the great room and climbed the stairway.

She could feel melting snow dampening the legs of her jeans and socks. A bit of snow had gotten down her neck and it, too, was turning to water. At the top of the stairs, she stood for a moment indecisively. Then she shrugged and opened the first door she saw.

It was his. Very masculine, heavy furniture made of logs, Mexican blankets decorating the wall. A pair of jeans lay in a puddle at the foot of the bed, a bridle hung from a foot post. The whole room had the look and the smell of the man who lived here.

Shivering, she crossed hardwood floors to fling open the closet door. A terrycloth robe hung from a hook just inside and she reached for it. It didn't look as if it had ever been worn. That thought made her smile. Dylan didn't look like the kind of man who would wear a white terrycloth robe anyway.

The smile slipped. Maybe he kept it handy for female guests.

Even if he did, she needed to get out of these wet things. Peeling off shirt, socks and jeans, she slipped into the oversized robe and belted it securely around her waist. Now all she needed were slippers but what were the chances of finding those?

Turning, she hurried out of his room and ran lightly back down the stairs. She'd been frightened there for a few minutes out in the snow alone but she no longer had anything to fear.

Well, not *that* kind of fear, anyway.

Dylan took his time working on the horse. Not only did the animal deserve the consideration, but the man wasn't all that eager to go inside the house until he'd had a chance to get a handle on his anger.

Damn-fool woman would have killed herself! She'd been wandering around in a raging snowstorm like any tenderfoot. She needed to be taught a lesson and he was just the man to do it.

Finally, when he could find no further reason to delay, he walked the short distance to the house. He took his time about hanging up his coat and hat, banging the snow off his boots, brushing himself off. Then he took a deep breath, squared his shoulders and walked into the great room completely prepared to rip into her good.

He saw her and stopped short. She sat on the leather sofa, her legs curled under her, the whole wrapped in his mother's white terry robe, the one she'd forgotten to pack when she moved to Florida.

Katy looked up at his entrance with a smile that quickly faded. "What's wrong?" she asked. "You look so grim."

"Are you really dumb enough not to know?" He stomped to the sofa and stood glaring down at her.

"Apparently." She looked completely vulnerable sitting there enveloped in white terry. "D-Dylan, I want to thank you for coming after me."

He gave a disparaging grunt. "Heck, it was nothing. I just saved your life, that's all."

She uttered an incredulous laugh. "Come on, don't exaggerate. You did a very nice thing, but I'd have made it without you."

"Really? Which way is the ranch house from where you ran your car into the ditch?"

She pondered. "North. And I didn't run my car into the ditch, I hit the brakes to avoid a deer and skidded in."

"Same difference. Tell me this, if the house was north, why were you walking west?"

She laughed. "Don't be ridiculous. I was following the road."

"No, you weren't."

"I...weren't?"

"You'd wandered off the road and were heading across country. If I hadn't come after you, we'd have found you frozen stiff as a poker some time next spring."

She stared at him, green eyes wide. "Do you mean it or are you just trying to get even with me for—"

"Dammit, Katy! I no longer have the slightest desire to get even with you for anything. I'm telling you that without me, you'd have been a gone gosling. Do you want coffee or cocoa?"

She blinked. "Cocoa?"

"You got it." He stomped toward the kitchen.

"Any marshmallows?" she called after him.

"You know the one about beggars and choosers?" he shot back without breaking stride.

In the big kitchen, he banged around looking for the things he needed: milk, a glass pitcher, cocoa mix. While the concoction heated in the microwave, he hauled down a couple of mugs, fighting to keep his thoughts at bay.

Mugs in each hand, he stomped back into the great room and stopped short. She wasn't on the sofa where he'd left her, instead standing at the window watching the relentless fall of snow.

She turned at the sound of his footsteps.

"I'm sorry," she said, barely breathing the words. "I do know better than to leave a car stuck in the snow, but the house seemed so close. I didn't think it'd be such a big deal."

He stared at her slender bare feet, thinking that they must be cold. His anger was spent, and in its place a new feeling crept, a feeling much warmer and much scarier.

"It could have been a very big deal." He spoke in a low voice. "Promise you'll never do anything that stupid again."

Her laugh sounded breathless. "You know I can't promise that. I do stupid things all the time, as you well know." She cocked her head. "Is one of those mugs for me?"

He nodded.

She held out her hand and he put a mug into it. "Be careful. It's hot."

"I always try to be careful," she said. "Sometimes it works and sometimes it doesn't."

"Try harder."

"Oh, Dylan!" Her laughter held a sad undertone. "Sometimes I think I'm too careful, sometimes I think my standards are too high, sometimes I think—" She stopped short.

"Finish your thought."

"All right." She tossed her dark hair back over her shoulder. "Sometimes I think I'm just destined to be alone."

"We make our own destinies." He carried his cocoa to the game table before the big window and pulled out a chair. It was easier to talk when he wasn't looking at her.

After a moment's hesitation, she joined him. Holding the mug between both hands, she sipped. "That's wonderful," she said. "And so warming."

"You're still cold, aren't you?"

She shrugged, looking almost embarrassed. "Just a little."

"Give me your feet."

"My—feet?" She looked at him as if he'd asked for something far more intimate.

"Your feet, and quit looking at me as if I was some kind of pervert. I can assure you, under normal circumstances there are other parts of your anatomy I'd prefer."

"My feet." She lifted one tentatively and he took it, resting the heel on his thigh. She lifted the second to join the first, still staring at him with a wide-eyed question.

Deliberately he began to massage her feet. They were icy but they quickly warmed beneath his hands.

She gave a little groan of satisfaction and slumped down in her chair, the robe sliding open enough to reveal a glimpse of slender thigh.

"That feels wonderful," she sighed. "Thank you!"

He lifted her feet and pressed them flat against his chest, wondering if she could feel the throbbing of his heart through her soles. He was, in fact, throbbing in other places as well.

Their glances met.

"Are you still mad at me?" she whispered.

He shook his head. "Are you still mad at me?"

"Was I?" She smiled.

He replaced her feet on the floor. "You left here fit to be tied."

"I guess I did. I'm not mad now, though."

"That's too bad."

Her brows flew up. "Why?"

"Because anger was the only thing standing between you and me and that bed upstairs. Now we're stuck here alone, at least overnight, and I intend to make good use of that bed."

"You do?" She looked mesmerized.

"Ohhh, yeah." He said it with his whole heart. "If you have any different ideas, say so right now."

She stood up abruptly, an expression on her face he'd never seen there before. "Where's the telephone?"

"In the kitchen." He, too, rose. "Are you calling for help?"

"I'm calling to say I won't be home tonight and don't worry—have the party without me." She reached out to brush her fingertips across his lips. "I'm going to tell them that I'm about to get a really special present I've waited for for a long, long time."

She took a few steps toward the kitchen, then looked back at him across her shoulder. "Don't make a liar out of me, Dylan."

CHAPTER TEN

KATY STOOD THERE in Dylan's kitchen holding the telephone to her ear and staring at him, standing in the doorway. The very air seemed to crackle with electricity.

She blinked back to the business at hand. "I'm fine, Grandma. Everything is fine, I'm just snowbound."

"With *Dylan?*" Grandma demanded.

"I'm afraid so," Katy said around a smile. Somehow she couldn't seem to take her gaze off him.

"Afraid? If that's the truth," Granny declared, "then you're no granddaughter of mine. Don't worry, we'll have the party without you."

The line went dead. Katy hung up without her breaking eye contact with Dylan.

He started forward. "Is she all right with this?"

"She's delighted with this."

"That makes two of us."

She went into his arms and they kissed. She came up breathless, aching for more. "Dylan...?"

"What?" He nuzzled her neck, his hands moving inside the wrap closing of the robe.

"Will you do something for me?" She blew in his ear and he jerked in reaction.

"What?" His voice sounded rough and impatient.

"Carry me up the stairs."

"Do *what?*" He jerked back to stare at her. "Have you lost your mind? You got any idea how many stairs there *are?*"

"I don't care." She tugged at his top button. "Ever since *Gone with the Wind,* I've wanted to be carried upstairs like that. If Clark Gable can carry Vivien Leigh, why can't you carry me?"

"Are you going to pout about this if I don't?"

"Probably."

"Then let's get it out of the way now."

"Oh, good!"

She waited for him to scoop her up in his arms as he'd done on the horse. Instead, he picked her up and tossed her over his shoulder like a bag of grain.

She tried to wrestle her way free. "Hey, this isn't the way!"

"It's *my* way." He clamped an arm behind her knees. "If you're smart you'll hang on tight, honey, 'cause you're in for the ride of your life."

She sure was...and she loved every minute of it.

Dylan had just poured himself a cup of coffee the next morning when Matt pulled into the yard in his big red pickup, weighted in the back with heavy burlap bags of something; Dylan used feed but Matt probably used cement. Sipping, Dylan watched his friend jump out of the cab and plow through the snow toward the house.

Not too surprisingly for Colorado, the day following the blizzard had dawned clear and bright. Dylan had crept from bed only minutes earlier, unsure how

Katy was going to feel about all that had transpired between them.

Katy.

He turned away from the window and was pouring another cup of coffee when Matt barged in.

"I passed Katy's car in the ditch," he announced. "I take it she's all right, though. Grandma Andrews said she talked to her last night."

"Yeah, she's fine." Dylan offered the cup.

"You don't look too damned fine." Matt took the coffee.

Dylan shrugged, feeling an unexpected reticence to discuss what had happened with Katy—heck, he didn't *know* what had happened. He'd just wanted to sleep with her. He hadn't bargained for anything else.

Matt peered over the rim of his mug. "And Katy is…?"

"Still asleep."

"I see."

"The hell you do!" Frustrated, angry, Dylan began to pace. "We've made a real mess of this, Matt. I never should have—" He stopped short.

"But you did. You're a man. When opportunity knocks…"

"But now I feel like a louse. She didn't want to and I kind of made it impossible for her to say no."

"Katy?" Matt's brows soared. "We are talking about Katy Andrews, right? *No* is not a word she ever had trouble saying."

"This was different," Dylan said thickly. "There's this thing between us—sex, nothing more. We both knew this would be just a one-night stand—two at the most.''

"Isn't there a chance that it could be something more?''

How? Dylan wanted to yell. She wants a completely different kind of guy. *It's not enough that I want a wife and a bunch of kids and I want 'em with her because I love her*— He lost his breath and sat down hard on a straight-backed kitchen chair. He loved her but so what? She just wanted to pacify her family enough to give her time to find someone she could *really* love.

He drew a ragged breath. ''No,'' he said, ''there's not a chance in the world that it could be something more.''

Katy woke up alone.

Sunlight streamed through the window and lay in a golden beam across the hand-stitched quilt covering Dylan's bed. In her worm nest, she smiled and stretched luxuriously.

She didn't know where he was but wasn't worried. They were alone in this snug haven, safe from the storm. Perhaps by the time they were able to drive back to town, they'd have come to some understanding....

It was obvious they were in love. He couldn't have lifted her to such glory last night had he not cared for her as much as she cared for him. Today, she was going to darn well make him admit it.

Leaping from the bed, she dragged on the terrycloth robe. A cup of coffee was exactly what she needed. She ran from the room and was halfway down the stairs before voices coming from the kitchen told her they had company.

Matt. She recognized the low timbre of his voice, and Dylan's as he answered. At least it wasn't her brothers, she thought gratefully. If they'd found her here like this—

The voices became clearer as she approached closer and she heard her name. She shouldn't eavesdrop, she really shouldn't, but the opportunity was too tailor-made to resist. She'd just love to hear Dylan singing her praises!

She crept closer to the door, being careful to remain out of sight.

She heard Dylan mumble something, then say quite clearly, ''—sex, nothing more. We both knew it would just be a one-night stand—two at the most.''

Her stomach clenched. This was *not* what she'd expected to hear. Maybe she should sneak back upstairs the same way she'd come.

But she couldn't. She had to hear more.

''Isn't there a chance that it could be something more?'' Matt asked.

''No,'' Dylan said, ''there's not a chance in the world—''

Katy thought she was going to be sick. She'd made such a fool out of herself, thinking thoughts of love and commitment. She turned away blindly, knowing that she had to get out of here—now!

''Dammit!'' Dylan put down his coffee cup. ''Who am I kidding? I've at least got to try!''

''Try what?'' Matt looked interested.

"She may spit in my eye or laugh in my face but I can't let her just walk out of here thinking...what she's probably thinking."

"Which is?"

"That I just wanted to get her in the sack."

"Which you did."

"Yeah, but not *just* that. I also want—" Dylan choked on what he wanted. "Lots more than that."

"Then go get it," Matt advised.

Dylan took the stairs two at a time. He found her dressed and busy making the bed they'd destroyed the previous night. He watched her for a moment, thinking that only recently had he begun to appreciate how beautiful she was, how competent.

How cold, if he had to judge by the look she turned on him. What the hell was this?

"Good morning," she said, and she might have been speaking to a complete stranger.

He resisted the urge to reply in kind. "You okay?"

"Of course." She fluffed up a pillow and tossed it onto the bed.

"Matt's downstairs. He came to check on us."

"That was nice of him. I suppose you told him everything."

"Hell," he said, "I don't *know* everything. What exactly are you talking about?"

"Our one-night stand." She faced him with eyes like green chips of ice.

He couldn't help flinching. "That's kind of a harsh judgement," he said. "Last night meant a lot to me, Katy."

She laughed without humor. "Of course it did, but

there's not a chance in the world that it'll amount to anything more so why drag this out? If I had a magic wand—'' She sucked in her breath and for a moment her expression was vulnerable. "If I had a magic wand, I'd wave it and make everything all right. But of course, you stepped on my magic wand and broke it into a million pieces, so that's out.''

"Hey, it was an accident.'' If she was trying to be funny, it wasn't working.

"My life seems to careen from one accident to the next,'' she said.

"You want me to go out and come in again so we can start over?'' he asked. "You seem so...bitter.''

"I'd hoped to get through our 'liaison' without letting this happen,'' she said.

"Getting bitter?''

"No, *sleeping* with you!'' A flash of the old fire surfaced, then was quickly gone. "I'm annoyed with myself, that's all. Don't give it a thought.'' She started for the door. "I'm ready. I can go back into town with Matt and spare you the trip.''

"Dammit, I don't want to be spared the trip!'' He caught her arm and swung her around to face him.

Her cool look didn't warm by so much as a degree, and he quickly released her. "Why not?'' she asked calmly.

"Well—'' he searched for an excuse. "I have to make things right with your grandma. Our deal—''

"We don't have a deal anymore. Now that Brandee's married, there's nothing in it for you anyway.'' She stuck out her hand. "No hard feelings.''

He had plenty of hard feelings, but he shook her

hand anyway. There didn't seem to be much point in arguing.

But he wasn't a coward. "I'm not going to let you face them alone," he said. "I'm going into town, too. We'll tell them the truth together."

"I'd rather you didn't."

"I don't give a damn about what you'd rather. That's how it's going to be."

For a moment she stared at him; then she shrugged and turned away.

Katy rode with Matt, Dylan following in his pickup. She didn't say a single word on the drive that Matt didn't force out of her. Staring into the snowy vastness of the mountains, she tried to steel herself for the ordeal ahead.

She'd have to tell her family everything; there was no other way. Why had she ever tried to deceive them?

The snowstorm obviously hadn't been nearly as severe in town as it had at the ranch. Streets were already cleared, and the resulting piles of snow were melting rapidly beneath a brilliant sun. The day was beautiful, but Katy didn't care.

With Dylan on their tail, Matt pulled up in front of her house and stopped. "We're here, I'm afraid," he announced.

She gave him a strained nod. "Thanks for the ride."

He shrugged. "Katy, don't do anything rash."

"Rash?"

"Give Dylan another chance. He—"

"I have nothing to say to or about Dylan." She flung open her door and guess who stood there? She glared at him. "Why don't you just go home?"

"Sorehead." He glared right back at her. "Let's go in and get this over with so I can."

"Fine."

Side by side, but not arm in arm, they marched up to her front door, flung it open and walked inside.

And their nearest and dearest sprang forward shouting "Surprise!"

Dylan felt as if he'd been kicked by a mule. Granny rushed forward to hug him and he just stood there like a fence post, wondering how they were going to get out of this one. Liz, Katy's mother, beamed at them. She was holding baby K.C. in her arms.

"You couldn't make the party yesterday so we carried it over until you could," she exclaimed. "And don't worry, Katy—we invited your boss so you wouldn't get in trouble."

John Reynolds waved from the back of the pack.

Dylan glared at Matt. "Did you know about this?"

"Are you nuts? You think I'd have let you walk into—"

Dylan couldn't hear the rest because of the people surging around them, leading them to the sofa, pressing them to sit, thrusting cups of hot coffee into their hands, demanding to know about their adventures— in the snow, of course!

He could see Katy's struggle. She'd intended to walk in here and tell the truth, the whole truth, and now she couldn't.

She managed a strained smile. "Dylan saved me. I got stuck in the snow and he rescued me and carried me back to the ranch on horseback."

"Ohhh!" Laura looked impressed. "How romantic!"

Dylan saw Matt give her a quick glance that said, *Lay off!* She looked startled but didn't press the issue.

"Ma," Mack yelled from the back of the crowd, "can we get at that cake and ice cream now?"

"Me, too!" Zach's little voice joined in. "I like cake!"

"Don't you boys ever think of anything except food?" Liz complained with a smile.

"Yeah," Josh joined in, "we think about weddings—so when's the big day, Katy? Dylan, when you gonna make an honest woman out of our big sister?"

Dylan felt the oppressive weight of their attention. "I—we—uh, I'm not—" He glanced helplessly at Katy. He had no idea how much he should say.

"We'll talk about that later," she said quickly. "Mom, I didn't have any breakfast so I think cake and ice cream's a great idea."

Grandma sat down on the couch beside Katy. "Liz, you give me that baby and go get the cake so Katy can blow out the candles," she ordered.

Liz laughed. "Mother, you've just been looking for a chance to get this baby away from me." Nevertheless, she gently passed baby K.C. into the loving arms of a grandmother.

Katy took one look at her beaming grandmother, burst into tears and ran out of the room.

* * *

She returned ten minutes later—humiliated, contrite, and red-eyed—to find a subdued crowd waiting. From the looks of Dylan, he'd been grilled pretty seriously.

When they saw her, they at least refrained from rushing her—except for Jessica. Katy gave the little girl a wan smile.

"Before anyone says anything," she announced, "I want to apologize to all of you. I don't know what got into me."

Grandma cocked her head. "You wouldn't be in a family way, would you?"

"Grandma!" Katy stared at the little old lady, horrified.

"Sweet pea, I wasn't born yesterday. This is the nineties! Besides, you'll be getting married soon so what's the big deal?"

"That's just it," Katy said. She glanced at Dylan and saw the surprise on his face; apparently he hadn't thought she'd actually do it. "We won't be getting married. We never planned to get married. This was all just a stupid ploy to get you all off my back for another year."

You could have cut the silence with a dull blade, it was so thick. Expressions changed from loving and forgiving to outraged and confused.

Liz found her voice first. "Mary Katherine Andrews, are you telling me that you have *lied* to us about your relationship with this man?"

"I'm afraid…" Katy swallowed hard. "That's exactly what I'm telling you."

Dylan stepped to her side. "She didn't do this alone," he said staunchly. "We got into this for the best of reasons. It just hasn't worked out the way we thought it would.''

Mack's jaw thrust out at a belligerent angle. ''Just how did you *think* it would work out?''

''We—well, we—Katy?'' He deferred to her.

''We thought it would bring some happiness to Grandma in her...well, in her declining years.''

''Declining years, my eye!'' Grandma glared at her granddaughter. ''You thought I was on my last leg, so to speak, and you wanted me to die happy. Is that it?''

''Grandma, I don't want you to die at all, not ever!'' Katy hugged the little woman. ''I want you to *live*—and be happy. Since all you seem to want from me is grandchildren, and since I don't seem to have any luck finding a father for them, Dylan agreed to...well, to pretend. We didn't mean any harm.''

''They didn't, Mrs. Andrews.'' Laura tried to ease the tension.

''You knew about this?'' Grandma demanded.

''Well, yes.'' Laura glanced at Matt for support. ''We both did.''

''And you *encouraged* it?''

''Yes, we did!'' Laura's chin rose defiantly. ''Deep down, we were hoping that they'd realize that they really do care for each other and 'pretend' would turn into the real thing.''

Liz said softly, ''But that didn't happen.''

''No.'' The word hurt Katy's heart.

Granny pursed her lips. ''Balderdash!'' she announced. ''You two are the perfect couple, it's plain as the nose on my face. Besides, nobody else would put up with either one of you!''

Katy gave a shaky laugh. ''That may be true but—'' She glanced around, suddenly aware that the solid presence at her shoulder was no longer there. ''Dylan? Where's Dylan?''

Nobody seemed to know. Jessica dashed to the window and looked out. ''He's leaving,'' she yelled. ''He can't do that! Stop him, Aunt Katy!''

Katy wanted to so very badly. Everyone was looking at her, waiting to see what she'd do.

Except for Josh, a man of action. ''Want me to bring him back?'' he offered.

She shook her head. ''It won't do any good if you have to force him.''

Granny grabbed Katy's hand and squeezed. ''Tell the truth,'' she urged. ''You love that boy, don't you?''

All that love Granny seemed to sense welled up in Katy's soul and she couldn't have lied if there'd been a gun to her head. ''Yes, but he doesn't love *me*. He's sorry he ever got mixed up in this.''

''Ohhh!'' Granny banged her cane on the floor. ''You young people are not only blind, you're dumber than rocks! The boy loves you just as much as you love him but neither one of you has the gumption to say it right out loud.''

Jessica piped up. ''What you need is your magic wand, Aunt Katy.'' She added piously for the benefit of the rest of them, ''Uncle Dylan accidentally stepped on it and broke it into a bazillion pieces. I bet that's why they had all this trouble.''

Laura sighed. "You could be right, honey."

Katy gave a shaky laugh. "I'm desperate enough to try anything, but that wand is long gone."

"Which," Jessica announced, "is why Zach and I *made you another one for your birthday!*" She offered a long cylindrical package loosely wrapped in tissue paper and silver ribbon.

Katy stared at it. "Is this what I think it is?"

Jessica nodded eagerly. "It's even better than the last one!"

Which wouldn't be too surprising, since the last one had been made of a stick and a paper plate. It sure had worked, though. Katy tore at the wrappings. They'd gone all out on *this* magic wand: a dowel painted silver, a cardboard star glued and taped to one end, the whole covered with glitter that was already drifting to the floor in a glittery cloud.

At the window, Zach cried out. "He's starting his truck!"

"Now or never," Granny said softly. "You go, girl!"

It was time to grasp at straws—or magic wands. Grabbing up her special birthday gift, Katy went full speed out the door, flying across the yard to the curb. She could see steam coming from the front of the truck as warm air met cold, and she knew he was about to drive away.

Without hesitation, she darted in front of his truck, which lurched with his quick foot on the brake. Dashing to his door, she pounded on his window with her magic wand. Glitter dust drifted down.

Dylan rolled down the window. He looked haggard

and disgusted. "What on earth are you doing?" he yelled. "I could have run over you, you crazy woman!"

She socked him with her wand, right up alongside his head. "I'm stopping you from making the worst mistake of your life!" she cried.

"Which is?"

"Driving away from the love of your life, that's what." She whacked him again.

He tried to dodge the blow and failed. "Will you stop beating me with that stick?"

"No!" she yelled back. "I love you, you jerk, and my new, improved magic wand is going to make you love me back!"

Their audience, composed of Katy's family, Laura and her family, and the retired couple from next door who had heard the commotion and come out to find out what all the excitement was about, applauded.

Katy held her breath. Slowly and deliberately, Dylan opened the pickup door and stepped out into the snow and slush on the street.

"Let me get this straight." He took a step toward Katy, his gaze never leaving her face. "You love me?"

Jessica yelled from the crowd. "Everybody knows that, Uncle Dylan!"

Katy swallowed hard and nodded. "Of course I love you. Why else have I put up with you for all these years?" She swung her wand again and this time it hit his arm. "Magic, do your thing!"

Dylan froze. A look of fear crossed his face, followed by revelation. "I feel it working already!" He grabbed her in a bear hug. "Marry me or my life is over! Because I'll never find another woman who comes complete with her own magic wand."

And he probably wouldn't have, either.

EPILOGUE

SOMEBODY PUNCHED DYLAN in the shoulder and a voice whispered urgently in the darkness. "Wake up! I think it's almost time."

"Uhhh?" He rolled over in bed and automatically tried to take his wife into his arms. There wasn't much in this world better than having the woman you loved within easy reach every single night. "Time for what?" he mumbled thickly, nuzzling her hair.

"Time to go to the hospital."

For a few seconds, he just lay there; then he went stiff.

"Katy! You're sure?" He sat bolt upright in bed, then leaned over to switch on a light. He looked down at her, feeling wild-eyed and unprepared. "But it's the middle of the night."

She gave him a brave smile. "Babies don't care what time it is. They come when they want to come."

"Then don't just lie there! We've got to get moving."

"This baby won't be here in the next five minutes so don't panic," she reassured him. "I'm sorry I woke you but I just need company. I don't really want to go to the hospital until I have to."

"Why not?" He frowned and rubbed at his eyes, fighting his way through layers of sleepy confusion.

"I'll just call the doctor and tell him we're on our way."

"Not yet, Dylan."

"Why not? This is our first baby, Katy. The sooner I get you under a doctor's care, the better I'll feel."

Her pale lips trembled. "I know, you're just going to drop me off at the hospital and come back when it's all o-over."

He stared at her. "What gave you *that* idea?"

"We always joked that I couldn't melt you and pour you into a delivery room. It was funny then but now..." She choked back tears.

He couldn't believe his ears. "Mary Katherine Cole," he said sternly, "stop your snuffling." Jumping out of bed, he raced to the closet. "I was sure as hell *there* when we made this baby and I'm going to be *there* when he or she is born."

She stared at him with damp eyes. "You are? Even in the labor room and the delivery room? Oh, Dylan! You really do love me!"

Like she had to make a big deal about something so obvious. "You know damned well I love you," he said gruffly. "After all this time, you had doubts?"

"It was a test," she said happily, "and you passed. Now if you'll help me out of this bed, I'll get ready to g-go."

He could see the contraction bring stress to her face. Sitting beside her, he put an arm around her shoulders and held her until it passed. Then he kissed her cheek and helped her to her feet. She waddled into the bathroom.

Only then did he pluck her magic wand from its

place of honor on the wall above the headboard of their marriage bed. This was going to the hospital with them.

No use taking any chances.

"Get a move on, Katy!" He began throwing on his clothes. "No time to waste. I'm about to become a daddy!"

And from the bathroom, her response: "No, *I'm* about to become a mother! Honestly, Dylan!"

They argued about it all the way to Rawhide Memorial Hospital, where young Dylan Andrew Cole made his appearance only a couple of hours later at a healthy eight pounds and nine ounces.

And the baby was twenty-one inches long, exactly the same length as a certain magic wand which may or may not have had something to do with bringing the whole affair to a happy and satisfying conclusion....

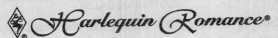
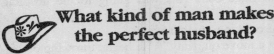

Come escape with Harlequin's new
Series Sampler

Four great full-length Harlequin novels bound together in one fabulous volume and at an unbelievable price.

Be transported back in time with a Harlequin Historical® novel, get caught up in a mystery with Intrigue®, be tempted by a hot, sizzling romance with Harlequin Temptation®, or just enjoy a down-home all-American read with American Romance®.

You won't be able to put this collection down!

On sale February 2000 at your favorite retail outlet.

Return to the charm of the Regency era with

GEORGETTE HEYER,

creator of the modern Regency genre.

Enjoy six romantic collector's editions with forewords
by some of today's bestselling romance authors,

**Nora Roberts, Mary Jo Putney,
Jo Beverley, Mary Balogh,
Theresa Medeiros and Kasey Michaels.**

Frederica
On sale February 2000

The Nonesuch
On sale March 2000

The Convenient Marriage
On sale April 2000

Cousin Kate
On sale May 2000

The Talisman Ring
On sale June 2000

The Corinthian
On sale July 2000

Available at your favorite retail outlet.

HARLEQUIN®
Makes any time special ™

Visit us at www.romance.net

PHGHGEN

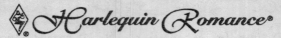